Ulla's Courage

Agnes Alexander

A Wings ePress, Inc.
Western Historical Romance Novel

Wings
Press, Inc.

Wings ePress, Inc.

Edited by: Jeanne Smith
Copy Edited by: Joan C. Powell
Executive Editor: Jeanne Smith
Cover Artist: Trisha FitzGerald

All rights reserved

Names, characters and incidents depicted in this book are products of the author's imagination or are used fictitiously. Any resemblance to actual events, locales, organizations, or persons, living or dead, is entirely coincidental and beyond the intent of the author or the publisher.

No part of this book may be reproduced or transmitted in any form or by any means, electronic or mechanical, including photocopying, recording, or by any information storage and retrieval system, without permission in writing from the publisher.

Wings ePress Books
www.wingsepress.com

Copyright © 2017 by Agnes Alexander
ISBN-13: 978-1-61309-717-5
ISBN-10: 1-61309-717-4

Published In the United States Of America

Wings ePress Inc.
3000 N. Rock Road
Newton, KS 67114

Dedication

To Aunt Helen Walsh – my most faithful fan.
Love you, Aunt Helen

* * *

One

Independence, Missouri
August, 1866

Two hours after her father's funeral, Ulla Wingate sat in the study with her Uncle Alton Wingate, his wife, Vida, and their daughter, Claudine, and waited as the solicitor prepared to read the will Grady Wingate had written. The two men who worked at Wingate's General Store stood in the background.

The solicitor, Shelton Barns, cleared his throat and began to read. *To my faithful employee, Wilbur Clark, who has been with me since the store opened, I leave the sum of two hundred and fifty dollars. To my other employee, Scottie Wells, who has been working for me for two years, I leave the sum of one hundred and fifty dollars.*

Ulla noticed her Aunt Vida frown and wondered why. Those men deserved even more and she wished she had known about the will. She would have encouraged her father to give the men a larger sum, but it was too late to add anything to the amount now.

Shelton went on. *To my brother, Alton Wingate, I leave the management of Wingate's General Store to be run as he sees fit. He is to draw a salary of fifty dollars a week for the first year and if the store continues to prosper, as it should, he has the right to increase his salary to seventy-five dollars a week the second year. For uprooting his family in Kentucky and moving to Independence to perform this service for me, I also leave him and his family my house and the contents, other than what belongs to my daughter, Ulla. My precious daughter will have the right to reside in the home until she marries and decides to move out on her own.*

This surprised Ulla, but she bit her lip and hoped nobody noticed how shocked she was. Without looking at her relatives, she continued to listen. She couldn't understand why her father would give her home away, but he had to have his reason. Maybe he thought Uncle Alton moving here was reason enough for giving away the house where she was born and grew up. The home she had thought would always be hers.

Again the solicitor's voice interrupted her thoughts. *To my beloved daughter, Ulla, I leave the ownership of Wingate's General Store, the savings account connected to the store, the continuation of the salary that I've paid her each week and the right to do with the store as she sees fit in the future. I do ask that she give my brother, Alton Wingate, the first chance to buy the store in the event she wants to sell it when she marries. Besides the store, she is to receive her mother's jewelry and any personal possessions she desires in the house.*

The short gray-haired solicitor looked over his wire-rimmed glasses at them. "That's pretty much it. I will give you a copy, Mr. Wingate and you, too, Miss Wingate. There is also a personal letter left here from your father to you."

Still in shock, Ulla nodded and took the letter the man held out to her. Though her aunt and uncle waited for her to read it aloud, she folded the missive and put it in her pocket. She had no intention of sharing her beloved father's last words to her with them or anyone else.

~ * ~

April, 1867

A thousand thoughts competed for attention in Ulla's head as she hurried to the bank with the money from the day's sales at the general store her father founded and she had helped run since her mother had died. Ulla had been twelve years old at the time. According to her father's will, she was the sole owner of the store, but for the past year it had been run by her Uncle Alton. By name, anyway. Though the public wasn't aware, she knew for a fact that her Aunt Vida made most of the decisions about what went on in the business. Not only did she work behind the scene at the store, she ran the household and everyone who lived within the walls of the home where they all had lived since the reading of her father's will.

Because of this, Ulla knew it was her aunt's idea that the money from the day's sales at the store be taken to the bank before it closed at five each day, though her uncle had issued the directive. She also knew Aunt Vida insisted the time should be sometime in mid-afternoon and no later than four-thirty. Since Alton didn't dare disobey his wife, he either took the money himself or assigned Ulla the job.

On her way to the bank, Ulla couldn't help smiling when she thought of the relationship between the two Wingate brothers. Alton was a nice looking man. He had the same dark brown hair and brown eyes his brother had. But there the resemblance ended. Grady Wingate had been a strong man who was in control of his life and always did the things he thought were right, but Alton was so afraid of his wife he jumped every time she spoke. When Ulla and her uncle were alone in the store, he never failed to tell her what to do and seemed to enjoy ordering her around, but when they went to the house it was a different story. Vida would open her mouth and Alton was as a small child—afraid to defy her in any way, he always did her bidding.

In the months her uncle's family had occupied her home, Ulla still hadn't figured out her cousin, Claudine. At times she seemed as submissive to her mother as her father was. At others she'd fight with Vida just like a tiger cub when it wants its independence.

And then there was Colton Blackwood, the son of one of Vida's distant cousins. Four months ago, Aunt Vida invited him to visit. A visit that was still in progress and Ulla didn't understand why. She wasn't sure how to take Colton. He didn't add to the household or didn't seem to be very interested in anything going on with the family, the store or even others in town. He was pleasant enough, but he was just there. And Ulla couldn't help noticing he was lazy.

After he'd been in the house a month, Alton assigned him to help Claudine with ordering stock, a job her mother suggested she be assigned earlier. When Claudine and Colton worked up an order, they'd spend some time in the stock room, but Ulla wondered how much ordering had been going on because she often heard them in the back laughing and giggling. Colton would also come into the store to work occasionally, but never helped out for a full day. He always said Vida needed him to do something at the house or Claudine needed an escort into town because her mother didn't want her going into town alone. Most of the time he hung around with the women of the family and had no interest in spending time with Alton or any of the neighborhood men, who had at first welcomed him to town.

Lost in thought, Ulla didn't hear anyone behind her; then someone tapped her shoulder. She whirled around, ready to hit the culprit with the money bag in her hand. Then she saw it was Colton.

"What's the meaning of sneaking up on me like that, Colton Blackwood?" She snapped, not bothering to keep her voice low.

"I'm sorry I scared you, Ulla, but I was afraid you'd get to the bank before I could stop you."

Still irritated, Ulla muttered, "So what did you want?"

"Aunt Vida sent me to the sweet shop. I wanted some of their special apple pie for supper. Then I saw you and wondered if you'd join me for an afternoon coffee."

"I appreciate you asking, but we're busy. I need to hurry back to the store."

"Then I'll come around at seven and walk you home so we can talk. That will be all right, won't it?"

Ulla didn't know what they needed to talk about and she could think of a lot of things she'd rather do than be escorted home by Colton Blackwood. But for the life of her, she couldn't think of any way to get out of it. Finally she muttered, "If you insist."

He tipped his hat with one hand and started to reach for her hand with the other, but she avoided the kiss on her fingers she knew he planned by grabbing the bank bag with both hands. If he noticed, he didn't say anything except, "Then I'll see you at seven."

Ulla nodded, turned from him and hurried down the street to the bank. For some reason, she was wondering why Colton began so many sentences with the word '*then.*'

Reaching her destination, she pushed all thoughts of Carlton into the back of her mind, took a deep breath and opened the door.

"Good afternoon, Miss Wingate." Ivy Nettleton started out the door as Ulla stepped inside.

"Hello, Miz Nettleton. How are you?"

Ivy gave her a weak smile. "I'm all right. And you?"

"I'm well, thank you."

Ivy nodded and hurried away without saying anything else.

Ulla wasn't surprised. Few people bothered to speak to Ivy Nettleton for several reasons. First of all, the woman dared to have a child out of wedlock. Then she had the nerve to let everyone know her baby's father was Peter Nettleton, who robbed the gun shop and was sent to prison for five years before he even knew he was going to be a father. When he was released, she openly married the man and for over a year, they'd tried to eke out a living on a small piece of land on the edge of town. Everyone seemed to be waiting for him to resort to robbery or some other crime so they could send him out of town again. One day when she was in the store, Ivy had confided to Ulla that she and Peter were trying to save enough money to leave town and start a new life somewhere far away. But so far they must not have been able to collect enough because they were still in town.

As soon as Ulla turned around, the bank's president, Stuart Roberson, spoke to her. "Hello, Miss Ulla Wingate."

"Hello, Mr. Stuart Roberson."

He chuckled. "I'm glad you came in. If you have time, would you please step into my office? There's something I need to discuss with you."

"Is it necessary we talk now? We're awfully busy at the store and I'm only here to make the deposit."

"Yes, Ulla, I think it's important that we talk. Please come this way."

Ulla felt she had no choice. She followed him into his office and took the chair he indicated in front of his desk. She didn't say anything, but waited for him to speak.

He cleared his throat. "Ulla, I've known you since you were a little girl. Your father and I were good friends, as were my wife and your mother. In fact, since we never had any children, I almost felt I was your second father."

"I felt that way, too. You know how much I loved your wife. I'm sorry she died."

"I know you are, but it has been almost a year now and I'm managing to go on with my life."

Seeing the sadness in Stuart's eyes, Ulla changed the subject. "If you remember, I used to call you Uncle Stuart and Aunt Edith."

He grinned. "I wouldn't mind if you still called me uncle."

She smiled back. "I could do that, but I almost want to call you Papa Stuart?"

He gave her a big grin. "I'd love for you to do that."

"Then what did you have to talk to me about, Papa Stuart?"

Still grinning, he said, "Have a seat and I'll tell you."

Ulla took one of the chairs in front of his desk.

He moved behind it and went on. "I brought you in here because I feel I need to ask you something."

"Of course, Papa Stuart... Or should I call you Mr. Roberson when we discuss business? And whatever it is, I'll be glad to answer anything you want to ask me."

"From now on, it's Papa Stuart, no matter what we're discussing."

"That's fine with me, Papa Stuart. Now, what is your question?"

"I don't want to stir up trouble with your family or butt in where I have no business, but I've been taking care of your personal account and the store's account for a long time."

He paused and she said, "I know this. My father trusted you completely and so do I."

He frowned. "Are you sure?"

She gave him a puzzled look. "Of course I'm sure. What makes you think I don't?"

"Your cousin and his wife were in here yesterday and he wanted to draw some money out of your account. He said you were unhappy about the way we were handling your money and had asked him to get it out of this bank and put it in another."

Ulla gasped. "I never did any such thing. I can't believe this."

"I assure you, I'm telling you the truth, Ulla."

"Oh, I'm not doubting you. I just can't believe Claudine would do such a thing."

He frowned again. "It wasn't Claudine Wingate who wanted to get the money. It was Colton Wingate."

Her mouth fell open and she barely whispered, "I don't have a cousin named Colton Wingate. The only Colton I know is Colton Blackwood. He's a distant relative of my aunt and has been visiting in our home for some time."

He raised an eyebrow. "I had a feeling something wasn't right, so I told them you'd have to come in if you wanted to draw out your money or make any changes in your account."

"I don't know what's going on or what to say about it, except what I've already told you. I trust you and the way things are done in this bank. I do want to stress that I don't want you to ever let anyone except me take money from my account. Not my uncle or my aunt and definitely not anyone claiming to be a cousin of mine."

"You can rest assured that I won't." He took a deep breath. "Since you've cleared up that situation, I may be speaking out of turn, but I feel I should let you know about something else that's going on."

She was puzzled, but nodded. "Please do."

"You know your uncle comes by here when we open at nine to pick up money you or he have brought to the bank the day before. He says he wants it so he'll have enough to do business for the day, which I certainly understand. But there's something that isn't adding up and I can't help but find it strange."

Ulla frowned. "What's that?"

"Lately, when you bring the money back in the evening, almost the same amount is in the bag that he picked up. When your father was living, the amounts always varied drastically, depending on the day of the week and even more so if there was a wagon train in town buying supplies."

Ulla frowned. "I don't understand. We sell a little even on slow days and I know there should always be more money by the end of the day, and of course we add what was hidden in the store at night."

"Do you count the money you bring in when you deliver it, Ulla?"

"No. If Uncle Alton doesn't bring it, he always puts it in the bag and gives it to me. I figured he has counted it." She frowned. "What do you think he's doing with the money?"

"I don't know, but there could be several things. He could be taking it home and keeping it himself. He could have opened an account in another bank that you know nothing about. He could even have a gambling problem."

She couldn't help smiling. "I can't imagine Uncle Alton with a gambling problem. Aunt Vida would kill him and he probably knows that. He's afraid of her."

He smiled. "Then I guess he doesn't gamble, but whatever he does, he's making sure there is little profit for you at the end of a month."

"Oh?"

"I'm not just saying that to upset you, but I feel you should know what he's doing. He'll have us put thirty or forty dollars in your account, but that's all. He says things are slow and that is all the profit there is for you. It makes me wonder if he isn't trying to run you out of the store for some reason."

This revelation added to the things that were beginning to make Ulla wonder what was happening to her father's store. "I have a feeling you might be right. At times I wonder if the best thing for me to do is let him have the store. The way he runs things, it is going to start losing money soon."

"If it does, I'm sure he'll need more money to stay open. He could come to me for a loan and if I turn him down, he could close the store and start another one here or in another town." He shook his head. "He could even come to you and want you to put the money your father left you back into the store. He'd probably try to make you feel you should give it to him to save the business your father founded. That way he and his family would be able to get their hands on what your father left you, plus what should be yours in profits."

"Do you think they'd really do that?"

He shook his head. "I don't know, Ulla. You know them better than I do. What do you think?"

She knew he was right, but didn't want to say so. This confirmed what she'd been suspecting for some time. Her so-called family was trying every trick they knew to legally rob her of everything her father left her.

When he said nothing else, she stood. "Thank you for talking to me, Papa Stuart. You've sure given me a lot to think about."

"You know I care, Ulla. Please let me know if I can do anything to help you."

"I will." She gave him a smile. "At least I know I can always count on you."

He returned her smile, walked her to the door and gave her a gentle hug. She thanked him again and bid him good-by. Walking back to the store, her mind was full of muddled thoughts with one exception. She knew she was going to have to make some changes in her life and she knew Stuart Roberson would be there to help her when she came up with the right plan.

~ * ~

Cord Dermott pulled the covered wagon up to the back of the hotel and parked it near another that was there. Jumping down, he saw six-year-old Becky running toward him, practically dragging her little brother, Will, along on his short legs. Will stumbled and fell, then let out a loud scream as he hit the ground.

"I'm sorry, Will, I'm sorry." Becky squatted beside her brother and tried to pick him up, though his kicking and screaming hindered her. "I didn't mean to pull you down."

Cord reached them and scooped Will off the muddy ground. "Don't cry; you're going to be all right." He tried to control it, but he couldn't keep the irritation out of his voice.

"I'm sorry, Daddy. I just wanted to show Will the wagon."

"It's all right, sweetheart. He'll be fine. Let's go find Hilda and get her to clean him up." He walked into the hotel through the back door and headed to the Lawsons' room. He knocked on the door that Hilda Lawson and her husband, Fred, occupied.

"Come in," came a yell from inside.

Cord opened the door. A middle-aged woman was sitting on the only chair in the room with some kind of catalogue in her hand. "Hilda, why weren't you watching the children?"

She glanced up at him. "They wanted to watch you drive up in the wagon. I figured they'd be all right."

"Well, get up and see if you can calm Will down. He'll need to be cleaned up, too. He's all muddy and he's skinned his hands and knees."

She stood and took the still crying boy. To the little girl, she said, "Come on, Becky, you can help me."

"I want to go with Daddy."

Cord shook his head. "No, honey. I'm going to find Fred and then we're going to take the wagon out to the campground where the other wagons are. Gather up everything you own in here because we'll stay at the camp tonight."

"Fred's 'cross the hall talking with that Masters man. Wouldn't surprise me if they ain't been nipping at the jug that old man brought in." Hilda took the still crying Will and headed to the bed to put him down. It didn't seem to bother her that she would get mud on the spread. "Pour some water in that pan on the dresser and bring it to me, Becky."

Becky hesitated, but Cord said, "Go on honey. Make sure she gets Will clean."

"All right, Daddy," she muttered as she moved to the dresser.

Cord left them to take care of Will and knocked on the door across the hall. A woman who looked eighty, but was probably only forty, opened the door. "What you want?"

"Fred. Is he here?"

"Sure, I'm right here, Cord." Fred waddled up. "What you need?"

"I've picked up the wagon and the mule team. I'm ready to get it out to the camp."

"I guess you want me to come with you."

Cord frowned. "Have you been drinking, Fred?"

"Jest had a little nip with Masters and his boys. Ain't no need to get your dander up. I thought I'd have a little drink today 'cause I don't figure there'll be much time for drinking once we get on the trail."

"I told you I didn't want you drinking and coming around my daughter. Has Hilda had anything to drink?"

"She was over here a while ago yacking with Masters' old woman, but I didn't see her drink nothing. 'Course she's purty good at hidin' it when she sips."

Disgusted, Cord snapped, "Go to your room and help Hilda get your things together. We'll be sleeping at the camp tonight."

Fred must not have noticed Cord's irritation because he asked, "Do we have to go out there today? I like staying in this hotel."

"If you don't go with me now, you'll not be going on this trip at all. Then you can stay here until you run out of money and they throw you out."

Hilda must have heard them because she jerked the door open and yelled, "Get in here, Fred. You don't think Cord is going to keep paying us if we don't do what he says, do you?"

"Ah, Hilda…"

"Shut up." She went across the hall, grabbed Fred's arm and pulled him in the door.

Cord followed Fred into the room.

Will had stopped crying. He was sitting up on the bed and Becky was beside him. Though he wasn't sure he wanted to, Cord went in and picked up his son. "I'll take the children and get the things out of my room. You two be out back with your belongings in twenty minutes. I want to get to the camping area before dark."

Thirty minutes later, Cord and his party was on the way out of town. Becky sat on the driver's seat beside her father; Hilda sat in the back of the wagon with Will beside her, and Fred had sprawled out in the wagon's bed and either had gone to sleep or passed out. Cord wasn't sure which.

Cord shook his head. He wished he'd spent a little extra time trying to find a more reliable couple to come on this trek with him and the children, but he'd been too impatient to wait. The Lawsons were one of the few couples to answer the ad he put in the Atlanta paper and after talking with only two other applicants, he hired them. Maybe he'd made a decision too quickly, but he didn't want to wait to leave. He knew had to have someone to look after the children. Especially after he decided he had to bring Will along. Of course, his in-laws tried every way they could think of to keep him from leaving Atlanta, but when their pleas didn't work, they refused to help him in any way. Though there were a couple of maiden aunts on his wife's side of the family that could have joined him to care for the children, they refused after a discussion with Cord's in-laws. He knew Otis Andrews, his father-in-law, had dared any of them to help him pull up stakes and leave town, and of course Otis' wife, Thelma, supported him in that decision.

Cord recalled the moment he'd told the man his plans. They'd stood in the newspaper office and as always, Otis was making sure the paper was ready to print. Cord had the type set as they had discussed earlier, but for some reason, Otis always thought there would be a mistake. Cord cleaned his hands on his apron and said. "It's ready to go."

"I'm sure you have it right, Cordell, but it never hurts to have a second eye on the process."

"I know you feel that way; that's why I've decided this will be the last paper I will be printing for you, Otis."

Otis frowned. "What are you saying?"

"I've been thinking about this for some time. I've decided that I'm leaving Atlanta. I'm going to make a new start somewhere else."

Otis looked confused. "Why would you want to do that? You have a good job here and Mrs. Andrews will always be there to help with the children."

"You know as well as I do why I've decided to go, Otis. I don't want to spend the rest my life where everybody looks at me as the poor soldier whose wife betrayed him while he was fighting a war. And she chose to do it with a Yankee lieutenant."

"Why do you refuse to see how it was for her while you were gone, Cordell? She was so sad and lonely and...."

"Hell, Otis. I know you accepted her treason as a debt she paid to keep the enemy from burning down your house. Well, I don't accept it. She was a traitor, not only to me, but to her country as well. I'll never be able to forgive her or forget what she did."

"I think you're wrong. You'll eventually get over Lisa's betrayal and find a new wife. Now that she's dead, you don't have to leave Atlanta."

When everyone in Lisa's family had finally realized Cord was serious about leaving the area, there was nobody left to help him. Neither could he call on the Dermott family because there wasn't anyone left alive he could call on. The Yankees had come through Georgia, burning, raping and killing and not only was his family home outside of town burned, but his parents were shot down in the front yard and it appeared his younger brother, Steven, had died in the fire.

After he returned from war, he was thankful that Lisa's family home wasn't touched. It took Cord almost the year after returning to learn why. That had been only a few months ago and it was the reason he decided to take the children and start a new life in the West.

At first, he thought he'd leave Will with Lisa's folks, but when he told Becky, she cried and said she wouldn't go unless her little brother came too. After thinking it over, he decided maybe he'd better bring the boy. After all, there was a chance that he was mistaken about the child's parentage.

Now here he was with the children and the Lawsons almost ready to pull out of town and head for Oregon with the wagon train that was leaving in a few days.

"Daddy." Becky's voice interrupted his thoughts.

He glanced down at her. "Yes, honey."

"When we get to Oregon, can I get a dog?"

Cord chuckled. "What kind of dog do you want, sweetheart."

"A black and white one."

"A black and white one, huh?"

"Yeah. One with fuzzy hair so I can brush it."

"Why would you want to brush it?"

"'Cause I would. I like to brush things and Will won't hold still and let me brush his hair. Miss Hilda won't let me brush hers either. 'Course, I don't much want to brush hers. It don't smell good."

"Maybe she'll wash it before we leave."

Becky took hold of his arm and motioned for him to lean down. He did and she whispered, "See if you can find somebody else to go with us, Daddy."

"Why, Becky?"

"Miss Hilda is no fun."

"Has she ever done anything to hurt you?"

Becky shook her head. "I just wish me and Will had somebody nice to play with. Miss Hilda is grumpy sometimes."

"I'm sure there'll be other children on the wagon train for you to play with."

"I hope so, Daddy."

Cord pulled the wagon onto the edge of the campground and found a suitable parking place. He jumped from the wagon and reached up to help Becky down.

Hilda climbed out of the back and stood looking around. "This ain't much of a place, is it?"

"This is the campground for all the emigrants getting ready to head west. It gives us all a chance to meet the other travelers and make friends. We're going to need them on the trail and Mr. Pruitt expects us to help each other when things arise on the journey that's too much for one family."

Hilda frowned at him and nodded toward the wagon. "Might as well leave Fred in there and let him sleep it off. He won't be no good to nobody till he gets over the hangover he's gonna have."

"Daddy!" Becky screamed. "Will is going to fall out of the wagon."

Cord whirled around and caught the boy before he toppled out. "You shouldn't try to get out by yourself, Will."

"He's little, Daddy. He didn't know no better."

Cord turned to Hilda. "Your job is to look after the children. If you're not going to do it, you might as well head back to Georgia and let me find somebody who will."

Hilda looked scared. "I'm sorry, sir. I know I've got to do better." She reached for Will. "Come on, boy."

Cord let her have him. "Since Fred is incapacitated, I've got to unhitch these mules and get set for the evening. There's some biscuits and meat I bought in the café in town. Fix me some coffee and we'll have it for supper. The children can drink water. Then I'm going to saddle my horse and go back to the general store and order our supplies."

"Where are the children gonna sleep?"

"If Fred hasn't sobered up by the time I leave, I'll pull him out and let him finish his nap on the ground. Put the blankets in the wagon and the children will sleep there."

"What about Fred and me?"

"I'll bring tents back from town. We'll be sleeping in them."

Hilda looked as if she were going to argue, but must have thought better of it. "Yes, sir," was all she said.

Two

Cord was surprised at how crowded Wingate's General Store was when he stepped inside. He'd hoped most people had come in to buy their necessities earlier in the day so he could get his supplies ordered and get back to the camp before dark. Becky was afraid of the dark and though he knew Hilda should know what to do with her, since his return from the war, he liked to be there when his daughter needed him. Will was too little to know or care whether he was there or not.

Looking around, he noticed the pretty young woman behind the counter. She finished with a customer then turned her back and leaned down. Because of Lisa's actions, he'd had his fill of pretty women, but he hadn't completely killed his instinct to look at them. He thought this creature with the dark blonde hair had a shapely backside as well as being pleasing to the eye from the front he'd seen as he walked in. He figured she had bent over to put money in a cash box. Most stores kept their cash boxes under the counter. He hurried over to stand by the counter. He wanted to be there when she turned around to rise up.

"Oh!" She looked startled when her face came up and was level with his chest. She blushed and pushed a twig of hair back in the twisted bun on the back of her head.

"I'm sorry I scared you, young lady, but I was just trying to be next in line to be waited on." He was surprised at the way her green eyes sparkled. He hadn't seen too many blondes with emerald green eyes, and hers were unique.

"I'm sorry I was startled, but I wasn't expecting anyone to be there." She took a deep breath. "I'm Ulla Wingate and I'll be glad to help you next."

"Thank you, Miss Wingate. I'm Cord Dermott."

"It's nice to meet you, Mr. Dermott."

"Likewise." He gave her a smile, fished the supply list out of his pocket and handed it to her. "This is what the wagon master gave me. He said it was what we needed for the trip to Oregon."

She glanced at the list and nodded. "How many are traveling in your party, sir?"

"Five." He had the fleeting thought to ask her if she wanted to come along and make it six, but he didn't dare act on that thought.

"Are there any children and what are their ages?"

"Two children. My daughter is six and the boy is almost two."

She nodded and returned his smile. "Then we'll say you need supplies for four." When his brow wrinkled, she added, "They recommend the amounts for adults to be cut in half for all children under twelve."

"I see."

"I notice you have some boots and clothes on the list. We have these items for the children, but it would help if you would bring them in so we can be sure to get the right sizes. Children tend to vary in size more than their parents realize. Also since the trip to Oregon takes at least four to six months, they sometimes grow into a larger size."

"I can bring them in tomorrow, if that will work."

She nodded. "That'll be fine. I'll have the rest of this all gathered and ready for you by midday tomorrow. Will you be picking it up or would you like for us to deliver it to the camp?"

He looked surprised. "You have a delivery service for your supply orders?"

"The store doesn't have enough wagons to deliver all we need to when a train is loading, but we have an arrangement with the livery stable. They have one man who does nothing but make deliveries to the camp."

"I can understand that. I guess the street would get awfully crowded if all the emigrants brought their wagons into town at one time."

"It certainly would."

"Then by all means have my supplies delivered. But you can mark off the tents. I'll purchase them this evening and take them with me. Also I'll get a mattress and a couple of blankets. How much will I owe you for what I'm taking and for what you'll gather?"

She tallied up the bill and told him the amount. "I didn't add the children's clothing or any you might want to purchase for yourself. When you bring them to the store we can get the correct sizes. Varying sizes are different prices."

"I'll do that, Miss Wingate, and I thank you for your help."

"I was delighted to help you, Mr. Dermott." He couldn't help noticing she gave him that brilliant smile again. He figured she gave it to all her customers, but for some reason he wanted to think maybe the one she gave him was a little bit special.

After he paid her, there was no more reason to hang around, though he'd have liked to. He bid her good-by and went out the door. He couldn't help being happy that he had a reason to come back and look at her again. He wondered if she'd be pleased to see him.

Cord Dermott, have you lost your mind? You're heading west to make a new life for you and the children. Just because this is the first woman to stir you in a long time, there's no way in the world you need to be thinking such things. No pretty woman can be trusted. Haven't you learned that yet?

He climbed on his horse and headed back to the camp.

~ * ~

At ten to seven, Ulla looked up to see Colton walk into the store. He swept off his hat and put a big grin on his face. "I told you I'd come to walk you home and here I am."

Miss Alta Walters turned from the material she was surveying and couldn't hide the smile trying to crease her usual stern face. "How nice of you, young man. A lady should never be walking on the street alone this time of evening."

"Thank you, ma'am." He gave her a smile. "You're a very wise lady. I wish more women thought the way you do."

Ulla bit her tongue to keep from asking the blushing spinster if she didn't think a woman should be out alone, what she was doing here by herself? Instead she said, "I'll be ready to leave at seven, Colton."

Miss Walters walked up to the counter. "I just can't make up my mind, Ulla. I'll take the threads I've already selected and come back tomorrow to choose my cloth."

"That will be fine, Miss Walters." Ulla began adding the items. "I'll put this on your bill."

"Thank you, Ulla. Now you be grateful this handsome young man wants to escort you home. He's very thoughtful."

Colton grinned. "Thank you, ma'am."

Alton came in from the back room. "Hello, Miss Walters."

"Mr. Wingate." Miss Walters turned, smiled again at Colton and went out the door.

"Since Colton's here to see you home, Ulla, I'm going to head on to the house."

"That's fine, Uncle Alton."

He handed Colton the key. "I've already locked the back door. Make sure the front is locked and remind Ulla to put the money box in its hiding place."

"Yes, Alton, I will."

Ulla couldn't help glaring at him. "If I can't be trusted to lock up the store, then why don't I go home now and you can lock it yourself, Uncle Alton?"

"Now, now, Ulla. Let's not get testy." Her uncle glanced at Colton, shook his head and muttered, "Women." He grabbed his hat and walked out.

Colton nodded and a knowing smile spread across his face.

Ulla wanted to slap him and her uncle both, but instead, took a deep breath to hold herself back. How could her uncle not trust her to lock the door and put the money away? She'd done it many times for her father and she could do it now. And how could Carlton be so stupid as to think she wasn't capable of taking care of this store? It made her want to turn against the entire male species.

"Now that Alton's gone, why don't we lock the door and leave, too?"

She frowned. "I'm supposed to stay here until seven o'clock, Colton. I don't cheat even for a few minutes. Even if I could get away with it, I would know what I had done."

"I suppose that's partly why I think so highly of you, Ulla. You're honest to the core."

She didn't answer. For some reason, in the last few weeks Colton had been almost overly attentive to her. He always arranged to sit beside her at meals and when they had attended church services on the last three Sundays, he'd escorted her into a pew and made sure he had the adjoining seat. He'd make sure he stood every time she entered a room. Now he'd come to the store to walk her home. As she thought the situation over, she couldn't help wondering what his motives were. She wondered also if it had anything to do with his trying to get into her bank account, but she didn't have the courage to ask. For some reason, she suspected it did. She hoped if she watched him and listened to his chatter, he'd eventually give himself away.

Ignoring him, she busied herself by straightening some of the merchandise and hoping nobody would come in at the last minute.

In a short time, Colton broke into her thoughts. "The clock says it seven o'clock. I'm going to put up the closed sign and you hide the money like your uncle said to do."

She started to inform him that her uncle wasn't acting wisely by insisting she take a secondary role in running the store, but knew it would only delay their departure. She was tired and all she wanted to do was to get home, eat supper and go to her room where she wouldn't have to see another Wingate or Colton Blackwood until the next day.

When they stepped outside, Colton locked the door, put the key in his pocket and offered his arm for her to take. She saw no alternative, so she took it. They walked without talking until they reached the block where the house was located. He broke the silence. "Ulla, I suppose you've noticed that I've begun to be aware of you as a beautiful young woman."

She frowned, but only said, "Thank you, Colton."

"You know I like you a lot."

All she could think of to say was that she liked him, too, though she wasn't sure whether or not she was telling him the truth.

"I'm so glad, Ulla." She said nothing and he went on, "Don't you think it's time we take our relationship a little further?"

She paused, looked at him frowned. "What do you mean?"

"Well, I like you and you like me, so I think we should become more than friends."

She jerked her hand from his arm and stared at him. She wanted to ask him if he'd lost his mind, but she couldn't come up with the right words.

He took her hand as they climbed the steps to the front porch. "What I'm trying to tell you, Ulla, is that I think we should get married."

"What?"

"I think you heard me. So, what do you think? Will you marry me?"

Before she could answer, he grabbed her and pulled her to him, and kissed her fully on the mouth.

She pounded on his chest and pulled away from him. "How dare you kiss me like that right here on the front porch where everyone can see?"

"I'm sorry, my dear. I was just so excited I couldn't help myself." He smiled at her. "Now come along and let's go tell the folks the good news."

"Wait a minute, Colton. I don't..."

He ignored her and opened the front door. He captured her hand and hurried her to the dining room. "Folks, guess what," he said almost before they were in the room.

Vida turned from placing food on the table. "What do you want me to guess?"

Colton looked around as Claudine and Alton came into the room. "What's all the noise about?"

Vida shook her head. "I don't know. Colton and Ulla came in all excited, but neither has explained why they are so happy."

"It's simple," Colton said. "Ulla and I are going to get married."

"Wait. I haven't..." Ulla started.

"Oh, my." Vida practically ran to them and threw her arms around Ulla. "This is wonderful news. You two are so much alike I just know you'll make a happy couple."

Alton frowned. "I didn't even know you were seeing each other."

"We're not." Ulla looked exasperated.

Claudine eyed them and muttered, "Congratulations." He voice didn't show very much, if any, enthusiasm.

Ulla tried again. "Folks, please. We are not..."

Vida ignored her protest, stood back and looked at them. "When do you want to get married? I hope you plan to make it soon."

"It will be soon," Colton said. "If we can make all the arrangements, I hope to marry her by the end of the month."

"Oh, my." Vida put her hand over her heart. "That means we must work fast."

Ulla was getting upset. "Please listen to me. We're not..."

Vida patted her hand. "Don't worry, my dear. Claudine you'll help plan everything, won't you, dear?"

"Of course, I'll help, Mother." Again she sounded as if she would rather do anything than help with a wedding for Ulla.

"Well, let's sit down and have our supper. We can discuss all this as we eat." She reached over and patted Colton's arm. "Don't you worry...I'm sure we can get everything together by the end of the month."

Ulla knew by the look on Claudine's face that her cousin wasn't happy with the situation, but for some reason she was going along with it. Ulla wondered if she should get the girl alone and tell her there would be no wedding.

But she didn't have a chance to work up her courage to say anything; she was bombarded with chatter. Everyone except Claudine seemed to be elated by Colton's news. This surprised her even more. Especially Aunt Vida, who she expected to object to her relative marrying. Instead, her aunt was the most enthusiastic of all. She could hardly believe the woman wanted to start planning the wedding right away.

After several tries to tell them that she hadn't accepted Colton's proposal, she gave up and let them talk. There was one thing she knew for sure. No matter how many plans were made, she'd not marry the man unless something drastic occurred to change her mind. And changing her mind was something she knew would never happen.

~ * ~

Cord turned over in his bedroll and tried once again to go to sleep. He was still questioning his decision to hire Hilda and Fred Lawson to go with him to Oregon. But he hadn't been able to find anyone else who wanted to pull up roots and head west. It had to be somebody without ties to Georgia and somebody that didn't have a family begging them not to leave. Had he made a decision too hastily? Would it have hurt him to wait a little longer to make this trek?

No, he couldn't wait. He couldn't stand knowing that Lisa, who he'd loved with all his heart, had betrayed him— and with a Yankee officer. It was more than he could stand when he found the letters she'd kept. Not letters from him, but letters from her lover.

Then he found a batch of un-mailed letters. Letters she'd written to him confessing her transgressions. Letters she'd never mailed to him. In them, she admitted to the affair and said all she wanted was his forgiveness. She'd even begged him in one of them, but he couldn't give forgiveness to her. Not even now that she was dead. It was after learning who her lover was and how he'd been the reason her home and her family survived the ravage burning of Georgia that Cord knew he had to get out of Georgia and all the family who had accepted Lisa's betrayal of him. After all, they'd told him that at least she'd saved her family.

He knew that the fact that the officer went back to his family in Connecticut after the war meant she didn't have to send Cord the letters. He just didn't understand why she hadn't destroyed them. But she hadn't and the war ended. Cord came home. Oblivious to all that had happened, he was thrilled to find his wife and his two children alive when the rest of his family had been killed. Becky was overjoyed to have her daddy back and one year old Will soon took to the man he'd never seen. Cord took to him, too. After all, he'd made it home for a visit a year earlier and knew this was when Lisa had conceived the little boy.

Then the unthinkable happened. Lisa and the children were on an outing in downtown Atlanta doing some Christmas shopping when a runaway carriage careened onto the sidewalk and killed her instantly. The children were saved because the nurse had them at a store window looking at the toys inside.

Cord was devastated. For a while he didn't think he would be able to go on, but somehow he did. He went back to work in the newspaper office his father-in-law owned and spent his free time with his children and occasionally with Lisa's family. It was on one of those visits to her mother that she sent him with his brother-in-law into the attic to get the three trunks of things that had belonged to Lisa. His mother-in-law had said she didn't have the heart to go through them, but she thought there might be some items he'd want to go through and save for the children.

Four months ago, on an unusually cold February Sunday, an unusual event occurred in Atlanta. It snowed. The snow lasted most of the morning and early afternoon, and left about two inches of the soft white flakes on the ground. The children had never seen snow and wanted to go outside to play. The nurse took them and that was the day Cord decided it was time to look through the trunks.

After his discoveries, it didn't take him long to know what he was going to do. He was through with Lisa, her family and with Atlanta. He'd read about the west and decided he would go there to live. The only thing he had to think about was did he want to take Will? His indecision was fueled by the fact that in one of the letters Lisa had hinted that her Yankee lover might be Will's father.

Now here he was in Independence getting a wagon ready to move as far west as he could go with his daughter and maybe his son. He hoped and prayed that one day he'd be able to be sure about Will. The child liked him and called him Daddy. He just hoped that sometime soon he could forget that the boy might belong to another man. A Yankee, no less. But would the doubt always be there? If so, there was nothing he could do about it. He'd just have to accept it and do the best he could.

A horse snorted and he turned over again. "Damn it, Dermott. Forget it and go to sleep. You have to go back to town tomorrow for the rest of your supplies and then you'll be ready to get on with your plans. You can't back out now. Even though you don't have the most reliable woman to look after the kids, she'll have to do. As for Fred, you need him, too. You don't know a thing about keeping a wagon in shape for travel and Fred, even with all his drinking, knows about that. After all, he worked for a blacksmith when he was young. That has to count for something."

Turning once again, Cord's mind finally slowed and he began to grow drowsy. It took a little longer, but finally he went to sleep.

Three

The next day was a busy one at the store. Not only did several emigrants come in to buy supplies, but several local people came too. One woman actually let her spoiled child rub her dirty hands on Ulla's skirt, but she ended up only buying the stick of candy the child had used as a weapon.

For some reason, Ulla was disappointed that Cord Dermott didn't come in with his children. She was looking forward to meeting them, but knew this was a silly notion. The man was headed west and she'd never see him again. Besides, he was a married man or he wouldn't have mentioned his children.

Between customers, she did decide she had to tell her aunt she wasn't going to marry Colton Blackwood, no matter what anyone thought. As excited as Vida had been about the wedding, Ulla expected her to try to talk her into going on with the nuptials, but that wasn't going to happen. Aunt Vida would just have to understand that her niece had never accepted Colton's proposal in the first place and she had no intention of doing so in the future.

Ulla debated with herself about whether or not she should tell her aunt that Colton had tried to get her money from the bank. But after thinking it over, she decided not to mention it. Vida could be behind that, as she was everything else that happened in the family.

Ulla stopped with the bolt of cloth she was replacing on the table after cutting a length for Miss Walters, who had returned to get her material. It hit Ulla that maybe her aunt was behind Colton's sudden proposal. But why?

"Oh, Ulla," Miss Walters' voice interrupted her thought. "What's taking so long to put that bolt of cloth back? I need to get on my way."

"I'm sorry, Miss Walters." Ulla turned with a smile. "I was just looking at the shelf of trims to see what would look pretty with this print."

"I didn't even think of trim, but of course, you're right. I will need something for the neck and the sleeves." She walked over to the sewing section. "What would you suggest?"

"Let me show you the ones I think would look good and you can decide which one you like." It didn't take her long to select three different trims and lay them on the bolt.

"Oh my. They're all lovely." Miss Walters turned her head to the right. "Which one do you like?"

Ulla pointed out the blue binding. "This one picks up the blue of the flowers and I think it would be lovely."

Miss Walters nodded. "You're right, my dear. I'll take three yards of that one."

Ulla cut the trim, carried it to the counter and added up Miss Walter's bill.

After the woman left with her package, Alton said, "That was smart of you, Ulla. I thought you were trying to get out of work by spending so much time in the sewing section, but you were actually trying to increase the sale."

Ulla didn't tell him that the boost in the sale was an afterthought. She only smiled and said, "Sometimes it's easy to add to someone's purchase if you make them see they need what you're offering."

"Good girl. I want you to do more of that."

"Yes, Uncle Alton."

There was a steady stream of customers for the rest of the day. Business only slowed during dinnertime, which most people in the area considered the six o'clock hour.

Vida walked into the store at six-thirty. "Hello, Ulla. I've come to join Alton. We're going to the party for the mayor. You were also invited, weren't you?"

"Yes, but I plan to go home and change clothes first."

"I see." Vida adjusted the beaded cape she had around her shoulders. "I was thinking today that you might want to check out the trunks in the attic and see if your mother's wedding dress is there and is useable. It would save you some time and money in getting ready for the wedding."

At the moment Ulla didn't have the courage to tell her that she had already been through everything in the attic and had moved what she wanted to keep to a trunk in the attic at the store. If there had been a wedding dress there, she would have seen it. There hadn't been one. She was saved from answering because her uncle walked in from the back.

"I see you're already here, Vida."

"Yes. I'm set to go to the party at the hotel. Are you about ready to close up?"

He moved to the door. "Yes, dear. I don't think anyone else will be coming in, but I don't want to be held up even if somebody does show up."

Ulla watched as he pulled the shades and locked the door. "I don't mind closing early today because I worked hard all day long and I'm tired." He looked at Ulla. "Are you going to the party?"

"I plan to. The new mayor was a friend of my father's. But as I told Aunt Vida, I need to go by the house and change clothes. One of the children in here today got sticky candy all over my skirt before his mother could stop him."

Vida shook her head. "Then, by all means, you must get a clean dress. We're beginning to circulate with the town's elite and we certainly don't want the mayor or his wife to think we're nasty people."

"I wish people would keep their young'uns out of here. A store is no place for children." Nobody said anything and Alton didn't expand his thoughts about parents bringing their children to shop. He walked behind the counter and took the cash box to hide.

Vida said, "Ulla, why don't you put on that pretty yellow dress of yours? The one Claudine wanted, but it didn't button around her. The one I didn't think I could alter to fit her without messing it up."

Ulla had no intention of wearing the yellow dress. It was meant only for special occasions and going to a party with her aunt and uncle wasn't special at all. But instead of arguing with her aunt, she said, "I'll wear it if it doesn't need pressing. I know you wouldn't want me to show up in a wrinkled dress."

Vida nodded. "I agree with that, but please try to make yourself presentable. I'm sure Claudine will look stunning and we don't want anyone to think we don't want you to look pretty, too."

Alton interrupted, "Ulla, we need to change our hiding place for the money. I think I'll use the other shelf tonight."

His wife looked at him. "Why don't you get a safe for this store, Alton? That way you'd have all the money you need and wouldn't have to run to the bank so often. I'd feel better if we had control over our money all the time. I've checked into the way business is done and I found that all successful enterprises have their own personal safes."

"You're right, Vida. I'll check into that tomorrow." He turned to Ulla. "Vida and I'll go on ahead. She wants us to be one of the first couples to the party. As Vida is always telling me, it's important to make a good impression on the people who run this town."

"By the way, Ulla," Vida said, "Claudine and Colton have probably already headed to the hotel for the party, so don't tarry. I know how you are when people stop you to talk on the street, but I can't stress enough how important it is we make a good impression. Our family hasn't been here quite a year and everyone doesn't know who runs things at the store now. And as you know, every important person in town will be there. I plan to invite most of them to your wedding. We can't have any of them thinking badly of us."

Why can't I tell her there will be no wedding? But I don't have the nerve to do it tonight. I promise myself I'll do it soon. She bit her lip to keep from blurting it out. Instead she said, "I'll be there as quickly as I can, Aunt Vida."

Though she wasn't looking forward to the party, she didn't want to do anything that would upset her aunt and uncle. She was still trying to work up the courage to tell them she wasn't going to marry Colton. After all, she and Colton hardly knew each other. Besides, she couldn't help remembering how much her father and mother had loved each other, and she was sure she didn't have those feelings for Colton and probably never would. He wasn't the kind of man who stirred her. A picture of Cord Dermott flashed across her mind and it startled her. Why in the world would she think of him? He was a married man with two children.

"Maybe it's only because he is one of the best looking men who has been in the store in a long time," she muttered and pushed thoughts of him out of her mind as she watched her aunt and uncle drive off in her father's carriage.

At home she hurried to her room and slipped out of the dress she'd worn to work and chose to put on the light blue checked frock with medium sleeves and a high neck trimmed with a blue binding. It wasn't as pretty as the yellow, but it wasn't ugly. He aunt should be pleased and if her aunt asked, she'd assure her the yellow one was too wrinkled to wear and she didn't want to take the time to press it. She combed her hair back into its bun and was about ready to step out of her room when laughter came through the wall from the hall.

She hesitated when she heard her cousin say, "Oh, Colton, I had such a wonderful time. I wish we could make love like this every day."

"I wish we could, too, baby. But when we can, I intend for my woman to always have a good time."

"How do you intend to make me have a good time when you're married to my serious old stuffy cousin?"

"You don't have to worry about my marriage to your cousin, Claudine. She's the type to want to work every day and I'm just the man to let her do it. That way I'll have my days free and I intend to spend most of them in your bed."

"What do you mean, mostly?" The pout in her voice came through the wall.

He laughed. "You know what I mean. Sometimes we might want to be out spending some of her money."

"Money that hateful old banker wouldn't let us get our hands on."

"I told you that would never work when we went to get it, but don't worry, sweetheart. When I marry her, the money will all be mine. She might think she'll be able to control it, but there's no way I'll permit that and, as you know, a man has control of his wife's property when they're married. That's why your mama said I needed to marry her."

"I just wish the banker would have let us have it. That way Mama wouldn't demand that you marry Ulla to get it."

"I guess she thinks it's the only way"

"I'm sure she's right, but I'm glad you'll have control of the money. Then if Daddy gets the store from her, she'll be at home all the time."

"Will you please stop worrying, Claudine. I'm make sure she gets involved in things to fill her time. Things that will tie her down and leave me free to spent all my time with you."

"But how will we ever be able to marry?"

"My marriage to her won't last long. I know it's not used much, but there is a thing called divorce. And I certainly intend to use it as soon as I get everything she owns in my name so your mama will be satisfied."

"Are you sure?"

"I'm positive, my love. Now, give me a kiss and let's get going. Your folks and your boring cousin have already gone to the hotel. They'll be watching for us and we can't mess up now and let either of them catch on to what we're doing."

"I know. Mother and Father would kill me for making love with you. She's always harping at me to save myself for the man I marry."

He laughed. "Well, in a way, you did. It will just be a little while before I can rid myself of Ulla, then you will marry the first man you made love to."

"Oh, Colton. I do love you."

Ulla didn't hear his answer because they had moved down the hall and the voices became only mumbled sounds.

Several minutes after the front door slammed, Ulla stood frozen in disbelief. So her aunt was behind all of it. She was even using her relative to get what belonged to Ulla. Besides that, in all her wild imaginings, a love affair between Claudine and Colton had never entered her mind. Though they had been cordial to each other, she would have never guessed they were more than friends. Was she the only one who didn't suspect? Did her aunt and uncle have any idea or did they know about the romance and condone it? Of course not. Claudine had said her mother wanted her to stay pure. This was something Colton and Claudine were doing behind everyone's back.

Ulla's first instinct was to burst into the party and confront the family, but her intuition told her that wouldn't be a smart thing to do. She now knew what her cousin and her so-called fiancé were up to, and though this was a shock, it didn't bother her that they were together as much as it would if she cared for the man. At least she knew she would never marry him, even if she had to expose them to stop the wedding. But the other revelation needed more thought. Claudine said her father was trying to get the store. What did she mean by that? And how could she stop her uncle, or did she even want to? She had a suspicion that under her aunt and uncle's leadership, the store was beginning to fail. If it did, Stuart Roberson was right…her uncle would expect her to give him everything she owned to get it back on its feet. Did she want it to come to that? And if she did give him her money, what guarantee did she have that once the store was again profitable, her aunt and uncle wouldn't think of another scheme to get rid of her? She wasn't sure what the answer to this question was. She was going to have to think about it.

Ulla dropped to the side of the bed and let her mind go over not only the conversation she'd overheard in the hall, but of the little things she'd heard in the last few months. She knew she needed to come up with a plan to cope with this knowledge in a way that was best for her and her future. Her father would want her to do that. He'd often complimented her on her brain. Now was the time to use it.

In a little while, the bones of a plan began to form in her mind, but it would take a few days to put it all together, then into action. In the meantime, she had to keep everyone from suspecting she knew they were plotting against her. Her first move was to get to the party and act as natural as she could. If they wondered why she was late, she would tell them she was held up by friends on the street and was late getting her dress changed. That way, nobody would ever know she'd overheard the conversation in the hall. Tonight before she went to bed, she'd make plans for what she needed to do next. She knew her best move was to take one step at a time.

~ * ~

The next morning Ulla was surprised when her uncle came downstairs behind her and said, "I'm not feeling well this morning. I'm giving you the key to the store so you can open up on time."

"I'm sorry you don't feel well," she said, though she knew he had a hangover. He'd drunk a lot a wine the night before.

"I'll try to come in by lunch time, but if I'm still not well, I'll see if I can get Colton or Claudine to come in while you take the receipts to the bank this afternoon. If they don't make it, get Wilbur to stay. I think I can trust him for the short time it'll take you to deliver the money. You won't have to go this morning to get any money. There's enough in the hidden cash box to operate the store today."

"I told you not to drink so much of that wine last night," Vida butted into the conversation when she came into the hall and followed them downstairs. "You know you don't handle alcohol well. When are you going to learn to listen to me?"

"Don't fuss at me this morning, Vida. I've got to get the key for Ulla, then I'm going back to bed. If you want to be useful, bring me a cup of coffee."

She ignored him and went on, "If I didn't think you'd be getting up for breakfast, I'd have slept late myself and now, since you said you're going back to bed, I'm going, too."

"So I'm not getting any coffee?"

"No." She turned to the door and headed back up the stairs.

"Will you make me some when I get up?" He yelled after her then grabbed his head.

"If I'm up, I will. If not, you can make it yourself." Her voice faded as she reached the top of the stairs and turned down the hall.

"Damn woman," he muttered as he went toward the study.

Knowing nobody in the house was getting any breakfast, not even coffee, Ulla silently followed him and waited.

He took the key from the desk and handed it to her. "Put it in the money box after you open up. That way, you won't lose it."

"I will, Uncle Alton."

He didn't answer, but turned his back on her and trudged up the stairs.

Though Ulla was hungry, she knew she could eat something at the store. It had been her good fortune that her uncle hadn't been able to resist each time a waiter came around pouring wine at the party last night. Now she had time to start expanding the plan she had in mind and putting it into action. She only hoped somebody would relieve her in time so she could meet with Stuart Roberson at the bank. She felt sure he would help her make the correct decision about what to do with her money.

On the way to work, Ulla had to pass the sweet shop. The smell of cinnamon hit her nose and she couldn't resist. She stepped inside and bought two buns. She knew if she didn't eat them both, Wilbur would probably be glad to get one.

When Ulla reached the store, she found Wilbur, the employee her uncle had retained after taking over the store, waiting as usual. "I'm sorry if I'm late, Wilbur."

"You're not late, Miss Ulla. Mr. Wingate told me I better be standing here every morning when he arrived or I'd end up like Scottie did. With a wife and four young'uns, I can't afford to lose my job."

"Uncle Alton isn't feeling well. He won't be in this morning, so we can both relax."

He grinned. "That's good news. I'm glad to hear it."

"I agree with you. It is good news. Let's hope his ailment keeps him home all day." She pushed the door open and he followed her inside.

"I've about finished gathering the supplies for that Dermott man. I saw the note that he wanted it delivered."

"Yes, but we'll be adding some things. He's coming in sometime soon with his family to get the clothes they'll need. He wasn't sure about his children's sizes. Hopefully, he'll show up today and you can mark that one off your list."

"Good. I'll be in the stock room if he wants to add the clothes and anything else to the delivery wagon."

"Before you go, would you start a fire in the stove? I'm going to make some coffee and I bought some cinnamon buns. Would you like a cup and a bun?"

He grinned. "I ate breakfast, but I sure would like another cup of coffee. I won't ever turn down a good cup of Arbuckle's."

Ulla nodded and moved behind the counter. She removed her hat and placed it on the shelf under the counter where she retrieved the cash box.

A local woman came in and bought a small sack of flour. "Had to get here before all those emigrants showed up. I'll sure be glad when they pull out."

"Yes, I'm sure a lot of people will be glad to see them gone." Ulla smiled at her. "Of course there's another train scheduled to leave in a few weeks. I'm sure they'll start preparing for their trip soon. You know the wagons leave continually from late April to June."

"I guess it's something you merchants do look forward to it since it means more money in your pockets."

Ulla only smiled, took the woman's money and bid her good-by. As she placed the money in the box, she had the woman's words about more money in her pockets on her mind. Was that what her uncle was waiting for? Did he plan to sell out of supplies to the next group of emigrants? Did he think there would be enough money for him to…to what? What was his plan?

Think, Ulla. Think. Your father always said you had the mind to solve problems that most people couldn't. Use that skill and decide what you need to do.

After eating one of the cinnamon buns and drinking a cup of coffee, Ulla felt better. Since it was a warm May morning, she took a cup of coffee to Wilbur in the stock room and then let the fire in the stove burn out.

The local dressmaker came in and bought thread and ribbons for the makings of a dress, but she didn't have much to say except that she needed to hurry back to her store and get started on the dress. It was for the new mayor's daughter, who would be celebrating her birthday soon, and she didn't want to be late with it.

Ulla was thinking about the problems she was facing with her family and straightening the candy jars on the counter when the bell over the door jangled a third time. She turned toward the door, then knew there was no use to try to concentrate on the problem of what she was going to do about her situation. Coming through the door was Cord Dermott. There was a small boy sitting on his shoulders and a little girl, who he'd said was six, walking beside him. They all smiled when he said, "This is Miss Wingate. She's the one who is going to help us get new clothes and boots for our trip."

"I sure will." Ulla smiled and wondered why there was a twitch in her stomach. Maybe it came from the cinnamon bun or the coffee. She usually had milk in her coffee. She came from behind the counter wondering why the children's mother hadn't come along. "Now who wants to try their boots on first?"

"Daddy first," the little girl said.

Cord laughed. "Well, Becky, I think there's some kind of rule that says a pretty lady goes first."

She giggled. "I'm not a lady. I'm a little girl."

"But I bet you're your daddy's little lady." Ulla reached for her hand. "So let's see what we can find for you."

She glanced at her father.

"While you're getting your boots, Will and I are going to look over the tools in that barrel in the corner." He winked at his daughter.

"All right, Daddy." She took Ulla's hand and followed her to the rack of children's boots.

Ulla looked into the little girl's eyes. Steel blue eyes, a little bluer, but still so much like her father's. With the child's blonde hair tied back with a strip of rawhide and her faded checked dress with a stain on the front, Ulla couldn't help wondering why Cord's wife wasn't more careful dressing her child to come into town. It would be different if they were already on the trail. One would expect children to get dirty traveling, but at other times.... What kind of woman was Cord Dermott married to?

Ulla was fitting the second pair of boots to Becky's feet when she whispered, "Could I try them on?"

"Which ones, sweetheart?"

"The white boots."

"Of course, you may try them on, but I'm afraid there's no place on the trail where you'd get to wear them."

Her face fell and Ulla wanted to bite the end of her tongue off and spit it out. She knew she was right, but a little girl couldn't be practical about something as simple as a pair of boots. Ulla grabbed the boots. "At least you can see what they look like on your feet. I bet your daddy will want to buy you a pair whenever you get to your new home."

Her attitude changed and she grinned. "He will. He loves me."

Ulla grinned back at her. "I'm sure he does."

"I love him, too."

Ulla was on the verge of asking her if she loved her mother, when the bell jangled and an older couple walked in. "Please look around and I'll help you in a moment," she said to them.

"Don't bother, ma'am. We came to talk to Cord," the man said and they moved across the room to where Cord and his son were.

"That's Miss Hilda and Mr. Fred," Becky whispered. "They're going to Oregon with us."

"Oh, really?"

"Yeah. Daddy said Miss Hilda is going to take care of Will and me 'cause he can't. Him and Mr. Fred will be busy taking care of the wagon and oxes and horses and stuff like that."

Ulla didn't bother to correct her pronunciation of oxen because she was busy wondering what Cord and the couple were talking about, but didn't want to eavesdrop. Cord and his friends deserved their privacy. She removed the white boots and put Becky's old shoes on her feet. "Now that we have the boots picked out, let's go over here and find you some dresses and socks and underwear and maybe a ribbon for your hair. I bet you'd like one, wouldn't you?"

"I wanted to put a ribbon in my hair today, but Miss Hilda said I'd lose it, so she used this piece of leather. I want to wear ribbons like Kathleen does."

"Is Kathleen a friend of yours?"

Becky nodded. "She come to our wagon and took me for a walk. She's a big girl, but she likes me."

Ulla was beginning to wonder why the child hadn't mentioned her mother. She wanted to ask, but didn't want to upset the little girl. "What's your favorite color, Becky?"

"I like red."

"You know what? I like red, too. Do you like any other color?"

"Blue. Daddy says it looks pretty with my eyes."

"I believe your daddy is right." She pulled out a dress made of medium blue wool. "How do you like this? It will make your eyes sparkle. And I have a blue ribbon that matches it. I'll give you one for your hair."

By the time they had all the clothes chosen that Ulla thought the little girl would need for the trip, she glanced up and saw that Cord, with Will still on his shoulders, had gone outside with the couple. There was nothing she could do, but go ahead and pick out clothes she thought would fit the little boy.

~ * ~

Though he felt a mixture of surprise and irritation, Cord tried to stay calm. When they got out of the store, he turned to the Lawsons. "Now, what is so important that you had to come into town to talk to me?"

"Mr. and Mrs. Masters come out to the camp and talked to us after you left."

When he said nothing else, Cord prodded. "And what did they talk to you about?"

Hilda put her hands on her hips and looked directly at him. "Fred will take all day to tell you, so I'm gonna do the talking. I don't like looking after your young'uns and Fred ain't excited about having to work on your wagon on this trip you say is around two thousand miles long and will take five or maybe six months. We're too old for that."

Cord's eyes narrowed. "But I told you all of this and you agreed to go with us before we left Georgia."

"I know that, but the Masters have found jobs here in Independence and they said they was sure we could get hired, too. We're going to do it 'cause we think it'll be a lot easier than going west in that bumpy old wagon you expect us to ride in," Fred said.

"Why the hell didn't you tell me this before we came this far?"

"We didn't know it would be so hard," Hilda said. "Your young'uns are more of a handful than I thought they'd be and I ain't never been one to want to look after squalling brats."

Cord was fuming, but he held it back. "Then return the money I gave you to go with me and get your belongings out of my wagon. I don't want you anywhere around the wagon when I get back to camp."

She looked at her husband.

He was trembling, but finally said, "We done spent the money."

"How could you have spent two hundred and fifty dollars?"

Fred looked at his wife and she looked away.

Cord knew they were lying and he grew angrier. "Then maybe I should ask the sheriff to hold you until you're able to pay me back."

Hilda looked scared. "No. I ain't told Fred, but I hid some of the money so he wouldn't spend it on rotgut. I'll give that to you." She started to scratch in her bag.

"You don't have to do that, Hilda," Fred whispered.

"Shut-up, Fred. We don't want to go to jail, do we?"

He shook his head.

She handed Cord about a hundred and seventy-five dollars. "That's all that's left. Fred's been spending some and I've bought a few things. I ain't got no more money and we done took our belongings out of your wagon."

Cord put the money in his pocket. "None of my supplies better be missing when I get back. If they are, I'll still have you arrested."

Again Hilda put her hands on her hips. "We ain't thieves and we didn't take nothing that belongs to you. We just got our stuff and left."

"Then keep going. I want you out of my sight."

~ * ~

The bell rang when he came back inside the store and Ulla looked up. Cord was headed toward them with an upset look on his face. The couple who had showed up to talk with him had not returned with him.

"May I speak with you a minute, Miss Wingate?"

"Of course."

He took Will from his shoulders, sat him in the floor and glanced at his daughter. "Becky, why don't you take your brother over there to the counter and look at those jars of candy? You can pick out one to buy."

Her eyes lit up. "Thank you, Daddy. Come on, Will." She took his hand and he toddled off with her.

Cord turned to Ulla. "I have a problem and I'm not sure what I can do about it."

"I don't understand."

"The couple that came in here were the people who had agreed to go on this trip to Oregon with the children and me. Now they've decided they don't want to go." She waited and he went on. "Without them, there's no way I'll be able to go. I can't manage the travel and looking after the children by myself."

"I don't mean to butt into your business, Mr. Dermott, but what about your wife? Can't she mind them or is she...?"

He interrupted her. "I don't have a wife, Miss Wingate. She died over six months ago."

"I'm sorry. I didn't know."

He didn't acknowledge her statement and changed the subject. When he spoke, it was as if he were thinking aloud. "Is there any way I can cancel the order for my supplies? I'll need the money to live on until I can find someone willing to make the journey west with us. If I can't find someone, I'll have to find a job and see if I can sell my wagon. Until then, I guess the children and I'll have to live in it."

It was as if Ulla's muddled plan suddenly became clear. She knew what she had to do, but she had to make sure she could pull it off. "Mr. Dermott, I happen to know a woman who I think would be willing to make the trip with you. She wants to leave town because her family has all died and she doesn't think she'll ever be able to find happiness here."

He raised an eyebrow. "Who is this woman?"

"I'll be glad to introduce you after I talk things over with her. Could you meet me at closing time? I'm sure I could have an answer for you by then."

"I can, but may I ask you one thing?" When she nodded, he asked, "How old is this woman?"

Maybe she had been wrong. This idea might not be the right one after all. He could only want a woman for his own pleasure. But if this were so, why did he have the middle-aged couple that came in the store set to go with them? "Does it matter what she looks like?"

"Not to me, but the wagon master would never allow a young single woman to travel with me unless she was my wife. He insists on families on his train. He says that way there is no conflict with the single men and boys trying to win a woman's favors. Of course, if she is older, he wouldn't object."

Ulla nodded. "I understand what you're saying, Mr. Dermott. May I ask you something else?"

"Of course."

"How badly do you want to leave on this wagon train?"

"I'd do anything, Miss Wingate, as long as it isn't illegal." He chuckled. "I'd even marry the woman, if that's what it takes."

Ulla raised an eyebrow. "That's good to know, Mr. Dermott. So let's plan our meeting. Would it be all right with you if I meet you at the café down the street at a little past seven this evening? That's the time the store closes."

"That sounds good."

"If you need to bring the children, it will be fine with me."

"Thank you. I'll see if I can get one of the women to watch them at the camp, but if I can't, I'll bring them."

"That sounds good. I'm sure I'll have an answer for you by then."

"I appreciate that, more than you can know."

"Daddy," Becky came running. Will was toddling behind her. "I picked out a candy. Can Will get one, too?"

"I guess he can." He took two pennies from his pocket and handed them to Ulla, then said to Becky, "Let Miss Wingate get whatever you two want. Then we need to head back out to the camp."

"All right, Daddy." Becky looked up at Ulla. "I wish you would come with us. You're nicer than Miss Hilda."

Ulla smiled at the child, but only said, "Thank you. Now, show me which candy you want."

Watching the man and his children walk out the door, Ulla couldn't help the feeling that she was watching her future go with them. Or was she only dreaming?

Shaking her head, she turned toward the stock room and called for Wilbur.

He came running. "Yes, Miss Ulla."

"I need to go to the bank... will you watch the store until I get back?"

"I sure will. Is there anything special I need to know?"

"Only if Claudine or Colton come in, tell them they don't have to work because you have everything under control."

"I'll do it."

"Good. I don't want them here this afternoon." She smiled at him. "I'm not sure when I'll be back. I have an errand I need to run and it may take a while."

"That won't be a problem. You know if we get busy, I know how to shuffle people around."

She laughed. "I sure do. Thank you for your help, Wilbur."

"You're more than welcome."

Ulla put on her hat, grabbed some of the money out of the cash box and headed to the bank. She was happy to find that Mr. Roberson was in and not busy. The teller ushered her directly to his office.

"I'm surprised to see you again today, Ulla."

"I didn't know who else to turn to, Papa Stuart, but I thought you'd be able to help me."

"Then please have a seat and tell me about it."

"I overheard a conversation between my cousin and the man who is visiting the family. I now know for sure that my uncle is trying to run the business into the ground. He wants it for himself and as soon as I pull out, he plans to use the money he's taken to open it again. I don't know if he'll do it here or if he'll go somewhere else to open up, but I'm sure he'll make money, just like he's doing now. Only next time he'll not have to take it off the top."

"What do you plan to do about it, Ulla?"

"I've made the decision to sign the store over to him."

He looked startled. "I don't understand."

"I have several reasons for my decision, so let me explain. First of all, they're pushing me to marry Colton Blackwell and that's so he'll be able to claim my money. Blackwell and my cousin Claudine are romantically involved and I overheard them say I was being used only as a way to the money my father left me."

"Are you positive about this or could you be mistaken?"

"I'm not mistaken, Papa Stuart, and yes I'm sure. As I said, I overheard them planning the whole thing."

"So you think by giving up the store, you'll be able to keep your money."

"Yes." When he asked how, she went on. "There's a plan forming in my mind that I'm pretty sure will work. If it does, it'll change everything that's been going on and it'll definitely change my life."

"Is this plan dangerous, Ulla?"

She shook her head. "Not at all. If I tell you what it is, will you help me?"

"I'll do anything I can to assist you, as long as I think it's going to be good for you."

"I've decided to leave on the wagon train that is heading out of town in the next few days. I've found someone who needs a woman to watch his children and I know I'll be able to do that because I love children. I hate to do this to your bank, but I'm going to take my money with me. I'd leave it here, but I'm not sure there'll be a bank where we're going and there'd be no way you could transfer it to me."

He looked thoughtful. "The money is no problem, but what about this man? Is he a good person? Is his wife along? I'm sorry to ask so many questions, but my concern is for you."

"I know that. He seems to be a good man. He brought his children in the store today for clothes for the trip. He seemed to be a very attentive father. His wife is dead and he had a middle-aged couple going with him to look after the children, but they've changed their minds and he's looking for someone to go in their place."

"A trip on one of those wagon trains is hard, Ulla. I'm not sure a city girl like you will be able to handle it. Especially with a stranger and his children."

"I'm aware of that. That's why I'm going to ask another couple to take a wagon and go along."

He raised an eyebrow. "Do you have a couple in mind?"

"Yes I do. Pete and Ivy Nettleton."

He smiled. "That's a good choice. They're really fine people and they deserve a fresh start."

"I believe that, too, but I have to ask them first. They may turn me down."

"I doubt that." He drummed his fingers on his desk. "Is there anything else you can tell me about this man whose children you'll be attending?"

"His name is Cord Dermott and the children are Becky, age six and Will, close to two. Other than the fact that I may have to marry Mr. Dermott so the wagon master will let me go, that's about everything I know about him."

Stuart looked startled. "Marry?"

She laughed. "Yes, marry. And believe it or not, I'd rather marry Cord Dermott, though I've only met him twice, than to marry Colton Blackwell, who I've known for several months."

"Marriage is a huge step, Ulla. Are you sure you want to consider such a step?"

"Yes. I'm sure."

"What if you do marry him and find you've made a huge mistake?"

"I don't think he's that kind of man. He seems only interested in his children."

"And he doesn't have a wife?"

"No. She died and he wants to start a new life in the west. He hasn't said, but I think he must have loved her very much and is making this move to get over her death."

"It seems you've spent some time thinking about this."

"I have. I know deep down it's the best answer for all of us."

Stuart nodded. "I know there's no way I can change your mind, is there?"

"No, Papa Stuart. I've decided that if Mr. Dermott thinks I'll be a good woman to care for his children, then I'm going to do it."

"If you're that sure, I think you could be right. That's why I'm agreeing to help you with your plan. I'll make sure your money is put in a strong safe box for you, if you think the cash will be safe. I'll also help you in any other way I can."

"I appreciate that. And don't worry about anyone taking advantage of me or my money. I don't plan to let anyone know I have the money with me. I won't put it in my trunk or any other obvious place. I'll hide it in a barrel with the bacon or something like that so nobody will suspect it's there."

"I see your ingenuity is showing and I'm sure your money will be safe."

"You're a wonderful man. I understand why you and Father were such good friends and I appreciate your help."

"You don't have to thank me. Your father was one of my best friends and if the situation were reversed, he'd do the same for my child. I'd do anything to help those he left behind."

For a moment, she thought about what the banker had said. She then sighed. "Papa Stuart, Wilbur Clark has been a faithful employee at the store for a long time. He has a family and if the store closes, he will be out of a job. Do you know anywhere he might find something to do that would be more secure?"

"You trust him?"

"Absolutely. In fact, he's in charge, since nobody is working in the store except the two of us today."

"Then tell him to come see me. I have a teller who is getting ready to move away. I'm going to need a good honest man."

"He'll make you a good employee. You won't regret hiring him." Ulla stood. "Thank you for everything."

"I'll have your money ready for you whenever you need it, Ulla. If there's anything else I can do to help you, please let me know."

She smiled at him. "There's one more thing I want to ask you."

"What is it?"

"If I have to marry Mr. Dermott, will you come to my wedding and give me away?"

He bit his lip and whispered in a cracking voice, "If you marry this man, I'd be honored to do that."

She knew he had tears in his eyes when he escorted her to the door, but she didn't let him see she'd noticed.

Four

Ulla knocked on the door of the shack at the edge of town and couldn't help noticing the startled look on Ivy Nettleton's face. Of course she'd expected the woman to be surprised to see her on the front porch. She gave Ivy a big smile. "I'm sorry to barge in on you like this, Ivy, but I need to speak with you and your husband about an important matter."

"Pete's in the back chopping wood. I'll get him." She looked as if she didn't know what to do, but she muttered, "Would you like to come in?"

"Yes. Thank you." Ulla stepped inside and followed Ivy to the kitchen. She took a seat at the rickety wooden table.

In a minute Pete came through the door. His son was at his heels. "Miss Wingate, I was busting up some wood for the preacher. He said he'd pay me and I planned to bring most of it to you to pay on our bill."

"I'm not here because of your bill at the store, Pete, and please call me Ulla."

He looked stunned. "Then why...?"

"I need your help and if you'll have a seat, I'll explain why I barged in without an invitation."

Pete glanced at Ivy, but she only gave him a puzzled look.

"You ain't gonna send my pa back to jail because—"

"Joe," his mother interrupted. "Why don't you go on back outside and start stacking the wood you father has split?"

"I've already stacked it, Ma."

"It'll be fine if Joe stays in here. This concerns him, too." She looked at Joe. "And to answer your question, young man, I am not here to send your father back to jail. I'm sure he'll never have to go to jail again."

Joe grinned. "I'm glad."

"Would you like some coffee, Miss Wingate?" Ivy asked, because she didn't seem to know anything else to say.

"That would be nice." Ulla noticed the good smelling soup that was on the stove and added, "I haven't had much to eat today."

Ivy looked as if she still didn't know what to say, so she simply poured Ulla a cup of coffee. She set one in front of Pete, too.

"The wife was about to call us in to eat dinner, Miss Wingate. Would you like a bowl of her soup? It's awfully good."

Ulla smiled. "Yes, I would like a bowl. It smells wonderful and I was afraid you wouldn't ask me to join you. But there's only one thing I insist on."

He lifted an eyebrow. "What's that?"

"I want you to drop the Miss Wingate and start calling me Ulla."

He nodded. "Then, Ivy will you please serve Miss Ulla a bowl of soup?"

"Of course." Ivy grabbed a bowl from the shelf on the wall, filled it and set it before Ulla.

Ulla took a deep breath. "I don't want to eat alone. Why don't you have your meal and we'll talk while we eat? And you can drop the Miss, Pete. It's just to be Ulla."

In a matter of minutes, the four of them were gathered around the table eating. It took a little while, but when they finally relaxed, Ulla told them why she had come to visit.

The three of them stared at her. Finally, Pete said, "So, what you're saying is if my family and I will join this wagon train and agree to help you and this Dermott fellow get to Oregon or wherever he's going, you'll arrange for the wagon and all the supplies we'll need for the journey."

"Yes, Pete. That's exactly what I'm saying. Since you've been doing odd jobs since you've been home, I know you have some experience with working with your hands on wagons and such. That will be a big help to Mr. Dermott. Ivy is a wonderful mother and cook, so she'll be able to help me mind the children and fix the meals while you men take care of the work you need to do."

"It sounds like a dream come true." Ivy had tears in her eyes. "I can't believe you'd do this for us, Ulla."

"Me either." Pete's eyes had the look of a man who trusted very few people and he wasn't about to get into something he didn't understand. "Why would you want to help us this way?"

"I'm actually being selfish and doing this for myself. You'll be helping me more than I'll be helping you."

Pete looked at Ivy. "Do you believe what she's saying?"

"Yes. I trust Ulla. She's one of the few people who was nice to me while you were away."

He looked back at Ulla. "If Ivy trusts you, I'll trust you, too. If you're really serious about this, tell us what do we need to do to get ready to go?"

"The train is leaving on Friday, so you'll need to go through your things and see what you want to take. Try to keep it to a minimum. There isn't a lot of room after the supplies are put aboard. You'll be carrying about a thousand pounds of food and merchandise. I only plan to take about four changes of clothes and one trunk with things that belonged to my mother and father."

"Should I bring some of my tools?"

She nodded. "That will be good. I'm meeting with Mr. Dermott tonight and I'll arrange for you to meet him. You can discuss what you have and compare it with his items. That way you won't have duplicates of some things and not enough of another."

"That sounds good."

Ivy butted in. "I've been teaching Joe some writing and reading lessons. Will there be room for some books?"

"Absolutely. I'd like for you to teach Becky, too."

"Who's Becky?" Joe asked.

"She's the little girl I'll be looking after. She's six. How old are you, Joe?"

"I'll be seven on my birthday."

"Then you should get along fine."

He didn't answer that remark, but he did ask, "Can I bring my dog?"

Ulla smiled. "The trip might be hard on him, but I don't see why he can't come along and try to make it with the rest of us."

Joe broke out in a big smile and jumped up. "I'm going to go tell…"

"Wait a minute," Ulla said. "My aunt and uncle don't know I'm leaving, so I don't want you to tell anyone that you're going on this trip. They might try to stop us."

His face fell. "I can't even tell Springer?"

"Springer's his dog, Ulla," Ivy said.

"Well, now, I'm sorry I stopped you. I don't see why you can't tell Springer. I don't think he'll tell anyone, do you?"

"I'll tell him not to."

"Then go tell your dog, but be sure to warn him that this is a family secret."

"I will. Thank you, ma'am." Joe ran out.

Ulla turned back to Ivy and Pete. "The only other thing I can think of is that you need to come into the store and let me fit Joe and both of you with a couple of pairs of boots. There's a lot of walking on this trip and it's recommended that everyone have two or three pair. We'll also need to get a few different kinds of clothes."

Pete frowned. "Ulla, this seems a lot like charity to me."

"Say that to me when we're a few hundred miles from here and you've repaired a couple of broken axles, shot half dozen rattlesnakes and wondered if we'd ever reach Oregon alive."

He kind of smiled. "You expect it to be that bad?"

"I've heard a lot of stories that run in that vein. I've also heard that when the goal is reached, some families thought they'd died and gone to heaven. I'm hoping for the latter."

"I only have one more question," Ivy said.

"What is it?"

"I spent a lot of time this spring putting up berry jams and peach preserves. Would it be possible to take them?"

"Ivy, if you don't take them, I'm not going," Ulla said.

They all laughed, then Pete promised Ivy and Joe would be at the store early the next morning to check out the boots. "She knows my size and can get whatever I need."

Ulla didn't insist he come to the store. She knew since his return he'd avoided going into town unless absolutely necessary. Because of the way he was treated, she certainly understood why.

~ * ~

Ulla remembered Wilbur telling her a week or so ago that the delivery man from the livery told him they had a converted wagon someone ordered, but it had never been picked up and he wanted to sell it. He'd asked Wilbur to let them know if someone came into the store wanting to buy one. She hoped they hadn't already sold it. She crossed her fingers and headed to the livery to see if it was still available.

The wagon had not been sold and it didn't take Ulla long to strike a bargain that was agreeable between the two of them. Hershel seemed relieved to get rid of the wagon and Ulla was delighted to have a wagon for the Nettleton family to travel to Oregon.

Back at the store she went inside to ask Wilbur if he'd mind staying late to help her pull the supplies to fill it. He was finishing up with a customer and turned as she came in.

"You look pleased with yourself, Miss Ulla."

"I am very pleased, Wilbur. Everything is working out, but I still need your help."

"Sure. Whatever you want me to do, you know I will."

"Could you start pulling supplies to fill a last minute wagon before you go home?"

"Sure. What and how many are going in this one?"

"Three adults."

"It shouldn't take me too long to get the order together. Will we be delivering it?"

"It's to go in the wagon the livery stable had for sale. We'll get it packed before it goes out to the camp."

He frowned. "If you don't mind me asking, Miss Ulla, what are you up to?"

She laughed. "I don't mind at all, Wilbur. I think it's time I told you about my plans anyway."

When she finished, he looked at her with disbelief. "I can't say as I blame you, Miss Ulla, but I'm not sure I want to continue working here with you gone."

"There's one other thing. Mr. Roberson at the bank has an opening for a teller. I recommended you and he said to tell you to come by and talk with him."

He looked stunned. "Really?"

"Yes, really. Why don't you go talk with him before the bank closes? It doesn't look like we're going to be bothered by anyone in my uncle's family and you'll have plenty of time."

"What about the order for the Nettletons?"

"You can come back and start on it before closing time."

"Miss Ulla, you're a wonderful woman. Your father would be very proud of you."

She blushed. "Thank you, Wilbur. That means a lot to me."

"I mean it."

"I know you do. Now, get out of here before you make me cry."

Thirty minutes later, Wilbur returned with a big grin on his face and Ulla knew he'd been successful in getting the job, but at the moment she had a customer and couldn't say anything to him. She only smiled and nodded.

Wilbur returned the nod and headed into the stock room.

She finished with her customer and planned to call Wilbur back into the front so she could congratulate him, but she didn't get a chance. Two emigrants came and she guessed they came for additional items they'd decided they wanted or something they'd forgotten. Ulla decided she'd try to get to know them. After all, if she was going to be traveling with the group, she needed to make some friends.

"Hello, ladies. I'm Ulla Wingate. How can I help you?"

"Hello, Ulla. I'm Naomi Guggenheim and this is my friend, Charlene Mahoney."

"It's nice to meet you both. If you don't think I'm being too nosy, could I ask why you're headed to Oregon?"

"Well, dear," Naomi said, "my husband is a doctor and he's been reading about the west. He decided he wasn't doing as much good in his medical practice in Pittsburg as he could in a rural area like Oregon. He's sure the folks out there need somebody to take care of their ailments."

"I think that's wonderful. Your husband must be a good man. Do you have children?"

Naomi laughed. "I agree he is a good man and yes, we have a set of twin boys. Esau and Ezra. They just turned eight and are all excited to be going on this adventure with us. I also have two teenagers. Eli is almost seventeen and Esther is fifteen."

"The twins are how we became such good friends," Charlene said. "My son, Carney, who is seven, has become friends with Naomi's younger sons. I also have a daughter, Kathleen. She's thirteen. So far, Esther and the little Dermott girl are the only ones on the train she's become friends with. Most of the other girls are either much older than she is or think they're too grown up to be her friend. Also she's a little shy."

"I remember helping Mr. Dermott gather clothes for his children. I thought they were wonderful."

"They are. I'm just not so sure the people going with them will be much of a help to him. When he's not around, the woman doesn't seem to care if the children are clean and well fed. Also, she doesn't want to be friends with any of the other women at the camp. I figure you should be friends with everyone. It's a long trip and we're all going to have to depend on each other." Naomi fingered the box of handkerchiefs on the counter.

"She's right, you know," Charlene put in. "Of course, everyone on the train that's met us thinks it's strange that we've become such good friends. You see, Naomi is Jewish and I'm an Irish Catholic, but when you start out on a trip like we're about to attempt, we think you need to be friends with everybody on the train."

"I agree and if you'll let me, I'd like to be your friend here in town. I'll make the third wheel on this friendship wheel of yours. I'm a Protestant."

Naomi laughed. "Then, Ulla, we're going to invite you to be our friend right now."

"I accept. Now, what can I get for my two new friends?"

"My husband wanted me to get some more bandages and ointments. He's afraid he'll run out if there are many accidents on this trip. I also think I'll take one of these lovely handkerchiefs. A lady needs a few pretty things, even going on a trip like this and I don't think the one with the blue flowers will take up much room, do you?"

Ulla laughed. "You're right. It won't take up any room."

"Then I'll take one, too," Charlene said. "I want the one with the pink roses."

Ulla nodded and decided she'd get the one with the yellow roses for herself and the one with the daisy design for Becky. If things went as she expected them to, she'd find something little and easy to carry for Will and his father later.

~ * ~

Ulla closed the store at six because there was no more business. She then spent a little while helping Wilbur gather items for the Nettleton wagon. At six-thirty, she said it was time for them to go home. "I'm sure your wife will appreciate you getting home at a decent hour."

"Thank you, Miss Ulla. I can hardly wait to tell her about my new job."

"I know she'll be delighted."

"She sure will, and we owe it all to you."

"Stop giving me all the credit. If Mr. Roberson hadn't liked you, he wouldn't have hired you. Now, let's get home."

"I'm not going to argue with you."

They locked the store and headed out.

Ulla walked quickly down the street and up the front steps to the house she once called home. It didn't feel like home now. It was just the house where she lived. The inside of the house was quiet and this seemed unusual. On a normal day, her aunt Vida would meet her and start asking why Ulla had left the story early. She went into the kitchen and saw Vida standing at the window, eating peaches from one of the crystal bowls that Ulla's mother had cherished and Vida used for serving food just to irritate her niece. Today she ignored her aunt's actions.

"Where is everyone?"

Vida's lip looked as if she were going to snarl, but Ulla knew this was a normal expression when her aunt wasn't in a good mood. "Alton's still in the bed. He had a rough day. Claudine and Colton went to visit the mayor's daughter. They're all getting to be good friends and they're helping her plan her birthday party. I'm sure they would've taken you if they'd known you were coming home early."

"That's fine. I'm too tired to go anyway. Besides, I'm hungry for more than a light sandwich. That's what the mayor's wife always serves when they have company. " She noticed there was nothing cooking.

Vida must have seen her glance at the stove. "I didn't cook any supper since Alton didn't feel like eating. You need to either find something to hold you until breakfast, or go to town and get something to eat at the café."

"The café serves good hot food and that sounds good. I think I'll go change clothes and go into town."

"Suit yourself." Vida turned and went out of the room with the bowl still in her hand.

After taking a fast sponge bath, Ulla put on her green striped dress with short sleeves trimmed in white lace. She combed her hair and decided to put part of it on top of her head and let the rest flow down her back. She'd been told she looked pretty when she wore it this way and she wanted to look pretty tonight.

As she went out the front door, Ulla couldn't help smiling to herself. She was glad she didn't have to come up with some excuse for why she was going into town to eat. She just hoped she wouldn't have to come up with some excuse for why she was in the café if someone recognized her and asked why she was there. Maybe she'd say both her aunt and uncle were sick. That should work.

~ * ~

Cord Dermott was sitting at a table on the side of the café when she opened the door and stepped inside. He stood and smiled as she approached. "Good evening, Miss Wingate." He held a chair for her.

She was sure his eyes lit up when he looked at her. Maybe he did like her hair down.

Slipping into the chair, she said, "I'm sorry if I'm late. It takes a little longer to close the store when you're working alone."

"That's no problem. I was early." He sat facing her. "They said the special was fried chicken, green beans, potatoes and corn. I decided I'd have a steak because I don't figure I'll get many good beef steaks if I'm able to leave with the wagon train."

"Then you should order a steak, but the chicken special sounds good to me. Aunt Vida can't fry chicken very well and I've loved it since I was a child. My mother was an expert at it."

"Then you must order it."

"I see you're drinking coffee. I think I'd like tea to drink tonight."

The waitress walked up and he ordered for both of them, adding, "Please bring the lady a cup of tea while we wait for our food."

"Yes, sir."

When they were alone again, he looked into her eyes and asked, "Well, are you going to keep me waiting all night to find out what you have to tell me?"

"I'm not sure where to begin." He said nothing, but kept looking at her. She wondered if she had been wrong about him thinking she looked pretty. Maybe he was only interested in the news she had for him. She took a deep breath and switched her mind from his enchanting gray-blue eyes. "There's a couple with one child within a year or so of your daughter's age. They want to go west and they're willing to work hard and follow instructions if someone will let their wagon go along with theirs. The man has some experience working on wagons and such and I'm sure he'd be able to fix anything that goes wrong with yours. The woman is a mother and I'm sure she'd be willing to help with your children when needed."

He smiled and she noticed the dimple in his chin. She looked away and he said, "That sounds good. I could use the help with the wagon and I'm good at telling people what to do. Is the woman willing to look after my children as well as her own?"

"She won't be looking after your children alone, but she's willing to help the woman who'll be looking after them."

He frowned. "What do you mean?"

She didn't answer because the waitress brought their food and said, "If you need anything else, let me know."

He nodded at her. "We will."

After she left, Ulla said, "I know I've confused you, but let me explain."

"Please do."

"When you told me the people who were going with you had decided not to, you said you'd do anything you had to do to leave with the wagon train on time."

"Yes, I said that."

"Did you mean it?"

"I meant it, but what has that got to do with anything?"

"It has everything to do with it, Mr. Dermott."

"Miss Wingate, you're still confusing me."

"I'm sorry, but please listen to me and answer my questions. It will all be clear shortly."

"All right. I'll try."

"You reiterated that you'd do anything, even if you had to marry the woman to get her on the train?"

"Yes, Miss Wingate. For Becky and Will and for a new start, I'd marry the woman if she wasn't too old or one who would mistreat the children."

"Even if you didn't love her?"

"I think it would probably be impossible to love someone you've never met, but that doesn't mean that love couldn't grow if the couple ended up liking each other."

The man seemed so sincere, Ulla just hoped she could depend on her instincts. Putting her fork down, she looked directly at him and mustered up all the courage she could. "I'm twenty-one years old. I've never been married or had children, but I like them and I'll never be mean to your children. And since I'll be the one going with you on the wagon train, do you think we should get married, Mr. Dermott?"

Cord dropped his fork and stared at her.

~ * ~

Of all the things this beautiful woman could have said to him, this was the most unexpected. Maybe he didn't hear her right. "What did you say?"

"I said, I'm the woman willing to go with you on the wagon train to Oregon, if you think I'm an acceptable person to watch your children and cook for you and them."

He still couldn't believe it. "Are you sure you know what you're saying?"

"I'm positive. So if you're not serious about taking me, I want you to tell me right now so I'll have time to find someone else I could go with on this wagon train."

Looking at her serious face, he realized she wasn't kidding. Still he wondered why she was willing to give up her easy living here to go with him on this journey. "I know you must have a good life here in Independence. Why would you want to go with a stranger and his children on a long, hard and dangerous trek to Oregon, Miss Wingate?"

"Does it matter why I want to go? Isn't my offering enough?"

"No, it's not." He gave her a crooked smile. "I'd like to understand this so I will be assured you won't be like the Lawsons and change your mind at the last minute."

"You're right. You do have a right to know and I'll tell you this much. My life here isn't as great as you might think it is. My father died last year and my uncle came to help me run the store. The problem is, he's changed everything and he's trying to take the business and everything I own from me. He's taking money that belongs to the store every day and trying to run it into bankruptcy so he can get his hands on what little money I have."

"How can he do that?"

"He and his wife have a plan to marry me off to his wife's relative. The fact that I don't like the man doesn't matter to them. So I've decided that I'm going to take what money I have and leave. If I don't,

I'm afraid my uncle will not only lose the store, but will run through everything my father left for me to live on. The couple I mentioned has volunteered to help me get away. They need a new start, too."

"Oh?" He wondered if he should ask why they needed a new start.

Before he could ask, she said, "I think you have a right to know. Pete Nettleton was arrested for robbery a few years ago. He spent five years in prison. When he was released, he came home to marry the woman he loved. She loved him as well, and married him over the protest of her family and in spite of the stigma of having his child before they could marry. They've been married for over a year now and though the town has shunned them, they have managed to stay together and find some measure of happiness with each other and their son."

He nodded. "I can understand being away from those you love."

"Well, Mr. Dermott, what do you think? Will you agree to the Nettletons and me going along on this trip with you and your children?"

He picked up his fork. "Then, Miss Wingate, I have a question I think you should answer."

"What's that?"

"I need to know your first name because I've forgotten what you told me."

Her forehead wrinkled and she looked confused. "Why?"

He chuckled. "I think at this point in our relationship it would behoove us to use first names. Mine is Cord, short for Cordell."

"I remember your name, Mr. Dermott. And to answer your question, I'm Ulla."

"Ulla. I like that." He was pleased to see her blush. It proved she wasn't as bold as she was trying to make him think she was.

"It was my grandmother's name."

He nodded. "What's our next step, Ulla? The train is supposed to pull out by the end of the week."

"Well, for one thing, you've bought supplies for two extra adults so I will have Wilbur pull one of them and add the clothes and essentials I'll need. Of course, I'll pay for my own things so you'll be reimbursed for the ones you've already paid for."

"No, Ulla. I'll buy the supplies you'll need. After all, I'm sure you'll earn them before we get to our destination. I've heard it's rough going on the trail."

She shrugged. "We'll discuss what I'll pay later."

He knew he'd lost that point for the time being, but he wouldn't push it. If she wanted to pay for her items, he wouldn't argue. He'd manage to repay her someway. He changed the subject. "We still have a problem. I have a feeling Mr. Pruitt is going to take one look at you and say there's no way he can allow such a pretty single woman on his wagon train with a single man without the benefit of marriage."

She blushed again and almost whispered, "I suppose that means you think we should get married?"

"Are you willing?"

She hesitated. "I thought I was."

He realized she was willing, but scared. He liked that she hesitated, but he didn't like the fact that she'd be afraid of him. He knew what he had to do, and he knew he'd keep his word once he'd given it to her. "Let me see if I can ease your mind a bit, Ulla. If it'll make you feel better, I will promise you that until you're ready to be a real wife to me, we will be married in name only. If that means we make the entire trip without consummating our marriage, then I can live with that because I already like you. I have a feeling that we'll fall in love and eventually have a happy and long lasting marriage, but I promise I'll not rush you."

He'd added the bit about love just to make her feel better. No matter how pretty she was or how much he'd like to take her to bed, he knew there was no place in his life for love. He'd had that once and it turned out to be a sham. He wasn't about to set himself up for that letdown again. Not even if they remained married for the rest of his life.

Her whole countenance changed when she heard his words. She looked relieved, satisfied and just a bit happy. "Thank you, Cord."

"You're welcome." He smiled at her and realized he was anxious to get to know her better, in spite of his feelings about love. But for the time being, he had to curb his enthusiasm about being with her. "Now that we have that settled, is there anything I need to do to help you get ready to leave?"

"I have a trunk in the attic at the store. I'd like to send it along with your supplies. It's the only piece of furniture I'll be taking. It has memorabilia from my life with my parents. I don't want to crowd the wagon with furniture we would probably have to discard along the way and would have to buy again when we get to Oregon. I also thought we should put a mattress in the wagon for Becky and Will. They're so young, I'm a little afraid to let them sleep on the ground."

"You've just now won my heart, Ulla. You're already looking out for the children."

"I want them to like me because we'll spend a lot of time together. I'm going to add a couple of surprises for them to your wagon. I hope you don't mind."

"Do you mind telling me what you're adding?"

"I thought I'd put in a tin of candy so when things get rough out there we can give them a little surprise to make them feel better."

"Good. I was afraid you'd say something like a pony."

She laughed, picked up her napkin and dabbed her mouth. "Speaking of animals, do you have a milk cow with you?"

"No. Do we need one?"

"Yes, I think so. The children are too young to drink coffee and they need the milk. Since I suggested it, I'll bring one. I know where I can find one that won't cost too much. Though the children will be drinking milk, it'll be nice for us grownups to have the cream to make butter. There's nothing like fresh butter on a hot fluffy biscuit. We can share what we don't use of the milk with some of the other travelers."

"So you can make biscuits?"

"Oh, yes. I make excellent biscuits and many other things. My father loved the food I made. I cooked for him almost every day until his death. I'll make sure we have a good Dutch oven to bury in the coals to bake them nice and brown. You'll be surprised at how well they'll turn out."

"I hit pay dirt when I got you for a partner, Ulla Wingate. Now let's plan how we're going to pull all this off in the short time we have left."

She nodded. "I suggest we finish our supper then have some of the apple cobbler they serve here and finish our discussion over dessert. The pie's wonderful and I'm sure you'll like it as much as I do."

"I'm sure I will." Cord wanted to tell her how lucky he felt he was going to be with her in the future, but he knew better. For the time being, he'd have to be satisfied knowing this beautiful woman wasn't only going on the trip west with him, but she was going to be his wife as well. Of course, he'd keep his promise not to demand she sleep with him, but he had a feeling it wouldn't be long until she would come to him willingly. It gave him more to look forward to. Not only did he have the chance to raise the children away from his former's wife's demanding family, but he was going to have a beautiful new wife to help him do it. At this moment, he wished they had everything arranged so they could pull out the next morning.

Five

The next day, Ivy brought Joe in to fit him in boots. Ulla had told her not to try to put them on her account if Alton was the only one there, but Ulla walked in the door just as Joe sat in the chair near the boots.

"I'm glad you finally got back, girl. Come over here and fit this boy in boots. I don't like putting boots on young'uns. They all usually have dirty feet." He glared at Ivy. "I've done told the woman she can't get no more credit until she pays off her account. She said she has the money, so be sure and get it from her before she walks out with them boots."

Ulla wanted to smack him, but she merely said, "Yes, Uncle Alton." She put her hat on the shelf under the counter and moved to the section where Ivy and her son were.

Alton pulled his pocket watch out and looked at it. "It's past my dinner time. I'm going to go home and get something to eat. Vida said she was going to make me some chicken and dumplings today and I sure like them. I just hope she isn't mad because I'm late and won't let me have any." He paused at the door. "You take care of things and I'll be back later, and don't forget to get that woman's money before she leaves. If she gets out of here with those boots, we probably won't ever see her again."

Ivy turned and looked at him. Her eyes said she wanted to shoot the man, but, in a calm voice, she said, "I'll pay you right now if you think I'm trying to get out of my debt."

"I don't have time to take your money now. Pay Ulla." Without another word, he walked out of the store.

Ulla moved beside her friend. "Well, Ivy. Forget him. Let's get this boy fitted in some boots."

Ivy was shaking. "Pete took out what money we had in the bank this morning. I thought I better pay off our account here even before your uncle said I had to. Do you want the money now?"

Ulla shook her head. "I've already marked your account paid, Ivy. Uncle Alton never looks at the books and he hadn't seen it was taken care of." When Ivy started to protest, Ulla added, "It's part of the condition for you and your family being willing to travel with me. You didn't owe that much anyway."

"But..."

"Don't argue with me, Ivy. You'll need your money later. Besides, I have this trip all planned out and I need it to go on as I planned it or I'll get confused." She turned back to Joe. "How do those boots feel, young man?"

"Great. I ain't never had a pair of boots this nice."

"I'm glad you like them." Ulla knew Joe would probably be rough on the boots. She selected three more pair and put them in a pile. "Now, Ivy, I want you to get yourself and Pete a couple of pair each and I'll help Joe find some suitable clothing." She moved to the counter. "What size shirt does Pete wear? We might as well get him a shirt or two, and maybe a couple of pair of pants while we're at it. You'll need a couple of wool dresses because they hold up better than cotton."

"We have some clothes we can take, Ulla."

"I know and I want you to take them. But clothes wear out quickly on the trail and I sure don't want to see any of my friends running around naked."

Joe laughed out loud and Ivy smiled.

By the time they had all the boots and clothes selected and Ulla sent Wilbur to take them to the Nettleton's wagon, it was after one. "When Uncle Alton returns, I want to ride out to the camp with you and introduce you to Cord Dermott. He's the man we'll be traveling along with."

Ivy nodded. "We'll wait for you at the house?"

"That'll be fine. I'll leave as soon as Uncle Alton gets here. I want you to go rent a buggy so it won't take us too long to get to the camp and back. Rent it for two days because we might need to take some things out to the wagon." She took some money from her pocket and handed it to Ivy.

"I feel bad about taking all this from you, Ulla."

"I'm delighted you're willing to uproot your family for me, Ivy. Material things mean nothing, but friendship is everything."

Ivy nodded and motioned for Joe to come along. "Let's get out of here before I start crying, son."

"All right, Ma."

"Just a minute," Ulla said. She went to the counter and took a peppermint stick from the big glass jar and handed it to Joe. "I always give a treat to the young men who come in and buy boots. It's their reward for letting me mess with their feet."

Joe's eyes lit up. "Can I take it, Mama?"

"Yes, Joe."

He looked back at Ulla. "Thank you, ma'am. You're nice and I told Springer about you."

"You did?"

"Yeah."

"What did he say?"

"He says he'll decide when he meets you, but I know he's going to like you, too."

"Well, you tell Springer I'm looking forward to meeting him."

Ivy smiled at her, shook her head and went out the door just as Alton was coming in.

"I hope you put that candy on her bill," Alton snapped.

"She paid off her bill and I rewarded her son with the candy. My father always did that when someone paid their account. I think it's a tradition we should continue to keep."

She knew Alton wanted to reprimand her by the way he chewed his lower lip, but he didn't say anything. She was sure she'd hear something about it later. It wouldn't surprise her if he made her put a penny in the till just to let her know he was still the boss.

"I'm hungry, Uncle Alton. I'm going to get something to eat, if you don't mind."

"Well, don't tarry. That wagon train is leaving the last of the week, but you know how those people are such poor planners. They'll wait until the last minute to finish shopping. I'm sure we'll get busy this afternoon."

"Unless something unexpected happens, I won't be too long." Ulla knew she was lying when she said it. She'd be lucky if she was able to get back before dark. She got her bonnet and went out the door.

She headed to the bank. When she'd gone by earlier, Roberson was busy and she hadn't had a chance to talk to him. She wanted to let him know she'd be picking up her money the next day and she wanted him to have it ready for her. Though she knew he'd already taken her money out and boxed it for her, she had to quash the slightest bit of doubt. He would laugh at her, but then he'd say she was smart to double check every little thing.

~ * ~

"Ulla, these chairs are great. Do you think...?"

Ulla laughed. "Don't worry, Ivy. I also put three camp chairs in your wagon. I know Joe won't be sitting much, but I met a couple of nice ladies at the store and I thought we'd have plenty of seats if we get a chance to visit on the trail."

"You thought of everything, didn't you?"

"I tried, but I'm sure I forgot something. Of course, it'll be too late to remedy my mistakes when we're hundreds of miles from here." She looked down the row of wagons and smiled when she saw Cord and Pete deep in conversation. "It looks like they're getting along fine."

"I'm so glad. Pete was worried because you told Mr. Dermott … I mean … you told Cord that Pete had been in prison for robbing the gun shop."

"I didn't want it to come up later."

"I see now that it was a good idea to let him know. Now there'll be no question if Pete gets moody."

"He does that?"

"Sometimes. I'm sure it's because he feels like everyone is looking down on him."

"Pete is not going to feel that way on this trip. I'm sure of it."

"I can't help but believe you, Ulla. Everything you've said so far has been correct."

Becky walked up, pulling Will behind her. "Can you watch Will for a while? I want to show Joe where the kids play sometimes."

"Sure, Becky."

Becky ran off. "Come on, Joe. It's down here."

Ulla looked down at the little boy. "Sweetie, would you like to sit on my lap?"

He shook his head and looked like he was going to cry.

She knew he wasn't sure of her and she needed to make him her friend somehow. She remembered the peppermint stick she'd eaten half of and put the rest of in her skirt pocket. "How about if I let you look in my pocket to see if you can find a piece of candy?"

His eyes got big. "Candy?"

"Yes, candy."

He hesitated only a moment, then put his hands on her knees and tried to pull himself into her lap.

She reached down and lifted him up. "Now let's see. Which pocket would it be in?"

He giggled when she held her left pocked for him to stick his hand in. He frowned when his hand came out empty. "No candy."

"You're right. There is no candy there." She turned to her right side. "Let's try this one."

He stuck his hand in the pocket and came out with the peppermint stick. He laughed out loud. "Candy."

"Well, what do you know? You found it. Now why don't you sit back and enjoy it?"

He scooted back in her lap and rested the back of his head on her chest. He popped the candy in his mouth and the leg that dangled to the side began to swing.

"Well, look a' here. It's my friend Ulla Wingate. What in the world are you doing out here?"

Ulla looked up. "Hello, Charlene Mahoney. Let me introduce you to Ivy Nettleton. She and her family will be joining the wagon train and possibly our circle of friends."

"Of course she'll join. Hello, Ivy. Glad to have you along. You got any kids?"

"I have a son, Joe. He's almost seven."

"That's great. I have a son who is seven, too. His name is Carney and he's over yonder in the young'uns play area."

"Becky took Joe over there," Ulla said.

Charlene looked at Ulla. "You know the Dermotts?"

"Yes."

"He's a fine man. I was sure sorry the folks that were going with him backed out. I've been trying to help him out a little. In fact, I came to see if he and his children would like to come and have supper with Liam and me. I cooked a big stew. Fact is, I've got enough for everybody. Why don't you come, too?"

"I'm not sure we'll be here long enough. I only came out with the Nettletons so they could meet Cord and his children. They'll be traveling along with him."

"Well, bless my soul. He found somebody to look after them. I sure hope you'll take better care of them than that Lawson woman did. She didn't pay them no attention unless Dermott was around. I felt plumb sorry for them." Charlene chuckled. "But since you have a boy of your own, Ivy, you know how to take care of children."

"Oh, I'm only going along to help out. Ulla will be the one taking care of Cord's children."

Charlene's eyes got big. "You're going on the wagon train?"

"Yes, I am."

"Well, glory be! How'd you wrangle that? Mr. Pruitt don't usually let pretty single women go on his train. Especially since she's planning on going with a handsome single man like Cord Dermott."

"Oh, he wouldn't have let me go either. That's why Cord and I are getting married."

There was no way Ulla could know, but before she and the Nettletons were back in Independence proper, practically everyone on the wagon train knew Cord Dermott was getting married. It gave them an excuse to have a celebration before they pulled out on Friday.

~ * ~

By the time Alton left for the mid-day meal the next day, Ulla had pulled and Wilbur had packed the final supplies needed for the trip in the Dermott and the Nettleton wagons. She'd had the wagon for the Nettleton family sent to the camp outside of town. Before sending Cord's supplies, as soon as Alton left, Wilbur took the trunk from the attic and added it to the Dermott wagon. While he was upstairs, Ulla had slipped out and buried her money under the bacon slabs and a barrel of potatoes. She would tell Cord about the money later. She learned the evening they had supper at the café that he was a proud man. She offered to pay, but he had insisted on paying for both their meals. She hadn't argued with him, but she knew from that conversation, he wouldn't want to accept her money as theirs. She'd have to spring it on him later and hope he'd change his mind. She felt sure she could figure out a way to for him to take it without hurting his pride.

When Alton returned from eating dinner, Ulla said, "Mr. Roberson wants to see you at the bank, Uncle Alton. I think most of the emigrants are through shopping. We aren't that busy this afternoon, so why don't you take the money and see what he wants?"

"I guess I might as well do that." He went behind the counter and put some of the money in the bank bag. As he went out the door, he said, "I shouldn't be long. He probably only wants to let me know we aren't making the money we expected to on these wagon trains."

Wilbur came into the store from the stock room. "I want to thank you again, Miss Ulla."

"I should be thanking you. You've done everything you can to help me get these wagons loaded without letting anyone know I was involved in the trip."

"I don't mind that, but I wanted to tell you I went to see Mr. Roberson again when I went to the livery to send the wagons to the camp."

"You did?" She smiled at him. "What happened?"

"You know, I told you already he hired me right the first day I went to see him. I know it was because of the glowing recommendation he said you gave him. Today he told me that I could go to work for him next Monday."

"That's wonderful, Wilbur. Mr. Roberson has been like a second father to me. He's a nice man and I know you'll enjoy working for him."

"I think I will, too, and now that I have everything done you wanted me to do with the wagons, I'm going to tell Mr. Wingate that I'm quitting. It wouldn't surprise me if he fires me today."

"He may do that." Ulla reached under the counter and took an envelope and held it out to him. "Just in case he does let you go today."

"Miss Ulla you don't have..."

"I know that, Wilbur, but you've been an asset to this store and you deserve it. My father would approve and as long as I'm part owner of Wingate's General Store, I have a right to give it to you. Besides, I appreciate you keeping my coming marriage to Cord Dermott a secret."

Wilbur looked in the envelope and his eyes widened. "I can't believe this. There's three hundred dollars here."

"I do have one other thing I want you to do for me, if you will."

"Anything, Miss Ulla."

"We're getting married tomorrow at four. Will you come to the church and drive my husband and me out to the wagon camp, then bring the buggy back to the livery? The Nettletons rented it for me and will use it to come to the wedding. I want to make sure it gets back to the owners before I leave town."

"I'd be honored, Miss Ulla. I'm sure you and Mr. Dermott are going to be happy. When he has come in to check on his supplies I've enjoyed getting to know him. He's a nice man."

"I think so, too."

The bell rang and Ulla looked up. Alton came through the door. He had a confused look on his face and she braced herself for his outburst.

He didn't waste time coming toward her waving a piece of paper. "Ulla, what the world do you mean by this?"

Wilbur butted in. "Mr. Wingate, I need to tell you something."

"Not now, Wilbur. I need to talk to my niece."

"I think you should listen to Wilbur, Uncle Alton. He told me what he plans to tell you. It's important."

"Oh, all right, he better be quick about it. What do you want, Wilbur?"

"I just wanted to tell you that I will be leaving your employ at the end of the week."

Alton frowned. "What?"

"You heard me, Mr. Wingate. I'm quitting. I'll finish up this week, then I won't be back."

"Why are you doing this? Don't you think I pay you enough for what little you do?"

"You're right, you don't pay me near enough for what I do, Mr. Wingate, but that's not the reason I'm leaving."

"So, why are you quitting?"

"I've found another job."

"So, just like that, you're walking out when we have the wagon train people coming in for supplies."

"I said I'd work until Saturday. The wagon train is leaving day after tomorrow."

Alton leered at Wilbur. "You'll be sorry. Nobody is going to put up with the way you slack off on the job like I've done."

Ulla could tell her uncle was going to become unreasonable, so she interrupted. "Why don't you go back to the stock room, Wilbur? I think my uncle wants to talk to me."

Wilbur turned to go and Alton yelled, "Yeah, and while you're back there, gather your things. Since the train is leaving Friday, I won't need you for the rest of the week. Ulla and me can handle it and if we can't, Vida has been itching to come in and help out."

Ulla was impressed when Wilbur turned around and walked up to Alton. "Then, sir, if you're making me quit today, pay me the money I'm owed for the days I've worked this week."

Alton looked shocked. "Who says I have to pay you?"

"I'm sure if I went for the sheriff, he'd say so. You can't work a man without paying him what he's owed."

"I think you should pay him, Uncle Alton. You don't want the sheriff coming in making trouble for us."

He took a deep breath. "I guess you're right." He moved to the money box and took out some cash and handed it to Wilbur. "You worked Monday and Tuesday, but only half a day today. You make a dollar a day, so here's two dollars and fifty cents."

"Actually I worked more than half a day today, but I'll let that go since you refuse to be a fair man." Wilbur took the money, stuffed it in his pocked, turned, winked at Ulla and left the room.

She had to bite her lip to keep from smiling. She knew the two dollars and fifty cents weren't important to Wilbur, but he had at last been able to say what he thought to his boss—former boss.

"Now, Ulla." Alton turned to her. "You need to explain things to me. I don't understand why you..."

The door opened and a mother and three children came in. "I want some candy," one child yelled.

"Me first," came from another.

"What about me? Mama, you promised me I could be first."

Alton sighed. "Oh, my. What next?"

"Don't worry, Uncle. I'll wait on them. I also see one of the emigrants coming in. I bet they've forgotten something. You need to wait on them and we'll talk after we close."

~ * ~

It was almost seven-thirty when Alton locked the door and pulled down the shades. "Can you believe we had to stay open half an hour after closing time? Why couldn't those people come in earlier to get the things they forgot?" When Ulla said nothing, he continued to rant. "Do they expect me to stay open all the time? My sign plainly says we close at seven o'clock."

"Aunt Vida would be wondering where you were if Claudine hadn't come to see what was going on," she mumbled, just to have something to say.

"I know. I hope she told Vida there was no way we could leave." He shook his head. "Did you see some of those crazy people standing around and waving their money? They were sure anxious to give it to us."

"It was good for business."

"I guess you're right. Now, quit trying to change the subject and tell me why you have decided to turn the store over to your aunt and me? You have never mentioned such a thing before."

Ulla knew she hadn't changed the subject enough that he would wait for her to explain things to him when they got to the house. She'd simply have to tell him why she gave him the store and get it over with. She opened her mouth to speak, but a loud banging on the door stopped her.

"We're closed," her uncle yelled.

Vida's voice came from the other side. "Open this door this minute, Alton Wingate."

He fumbled with the door and almost dropped the key. "I'm unlocking it, Vida." He pulled the door open and she stomped inside. If they weren't indoors, Ulla would have almost sworn her aunt had brought storm clouds with her.

"How long have you been closed?" Vida didn't lower her voice.

"I'd just took the key out of the lock. We finally got rid of the customers and were getting ready to start home. I wasn't going to take a chance on somebody else walking in and stopping us from leaving."

She glared at Ulla. "Is he telling the truth?"

"Yes, ma'am. Several emigrants came in to get forgotten items. I guess they were afraid to wait until tomorrow since they'll be preparing to pull out early on the morning after."

"It was a mad house, Vida." He glanced at his wife. "On top of everything, Wilbur quit today. Ulla and I had to handle it all by ourselves."

Vida frowned. "Wilbur quit?"

"Yes, he did."

"Why'd he quit?"

"He said he got another job."

"I told you that he probably would, since you cut his salary."

Ulla knew for a fact that Vida was the one who demanded Alton cut Wilbur's salary, but she decided to stay out of this conversation unless one of them spoke directly to her.

"But, Vida, he didn't do enough to earn what I was paying him. He thought he could hang out in the stock room and waste time."

"So you and Ulla were here alone?"

It suddenly hit Ulla that her aunt was jealous and she almost laughed out loud. How could the woman suspect her husband would be interested in his niece? In spite of herself, the thought almost made her laugh at the ridiculous idea of such a thing. Things were beginning to become clearer. It wasn't her uncle who was trying to get rid of her. It was her aunt. She now knew the woman had not only brought Colton there to marry her off so she could get her hands on the money her father left her, but she wanted her married because she was jealous. She couldn't help smiling inside when she realized how shocked her aunt was going to be when she realized what was really about to happen.

She plastered on a smile and said, "Aunt Vida, Uncle Alton was just about to ask me why I'd signed the store over to you and him today. I'm glad you're here so I can tell you both."

Vida looked surprised. "You did what?"

"It's true, Vida. I went to the bank because Mr. Roberson sent for me. When I got there he told me he had papers Ulla had signed giving me full control of Wingate's General Store."

Vida glared at Ulla. "Why in the world would you do that?"

Ulla was glad she'd already practiced what she planned to tell them. She only hoped she could make them believe her. "I thought about it for a while, and I felt it was the only thing I could do."

"That don't tell me a damn thing."

She was surprised at her aunt's cursing, but she didn't react. "Well, I got the idea from you."

"Me?"

"Yes. Do you remember when you told me how important it is for a wife to be at her husband's side?"

"That sounds like something I'd say."

"I've been thinking about your words and I realized you were right. A wife should concentrate on her husband and not be worried about how things at a store are running. I decided that after I was married, I didn't want to be working in the store every day, and I knew Uncle Alton would continue to run it as my father wanted. Of course, I knew Claudine was already doing the stock orders and I'm sure Colton will help out if he's needed."

Vida's face softened and she looked as if she swallowed what Ulla said. "I can hardly believe you've thought this through so thoroughly, Ulla. I'm proud of you for wanting to be a good wife, and I feel you're exactly right. Why, I'll even be glad to come in and help Alton with the store. I've been thinking that maybe I should anyway. I think running a store might be fun."

"I'd like to have you here, Vida," Alton said.

Vida might believe his words, but Ulla didn't. She could see the lie in his eyes, but she wasn't about to enlighten her aunt. "I'm glad you like the fact that I've given the store to you and Uncle Alton, Aunt Vida. I know you're honest people and you will keep putting aside my share. That way we'll all be happy and after all, all I want to do is please my family."

"Oh, Ulla, you have." She turned to Alton. "Now, dear, let's head home. I'll warm up supper for you and Ulla. Claudine and Colton were invited to visit with friends and they've already left, but I'm sure you two are hungry. We can have a nice talk about the part I can take in helping you run our store."

Ulla reached for her bonnet. "Since I didn't get to take the money to the bank this afternoon, do you want to leave it here or take it home with you?"

"I'm going to see that you order a safe to put our money in tomorrow, Alton. Then we can lock up the money before we leave every evening."

"You're right, dear. I'll order one. I guess we'll have to take it with us today."

Ulla got the cash box from under the counter and put the money in the bag so it would be easier to carry. "I think this is the most money we've made all week. It's a good thing those last minute customers came in."

Vida reached for the bag. "My goodness. It is a lot of money. Maybe I should carry it under my shawl. Nobody will see it there."

"That's a good idea, Aunt Vida." Ulla handed her the money and followed the two of them out of the store. She was pleased with how things had turned out. After tomorrow she felt her life would be on the right track for the first time since her father's death.

Six

The next day things worked out better than Ulla ever dreamed they would. Vida decided that since she was going to be running the store with her husband, she was going in to work for the day. "I want to see how things are done and how I might improve them," she said at breakfast. "Ulla can show me around, then she can take the afternoon off and concentrate on planning her wedding."

Ulla didn't correct her because in a way her aunt was correct. She'd plan her wedding, but it wouldn't be the one Vida was expecting her to plan.

Alton looked as if he didn't dare object to his wife's suggestion and Ulla was pleased. Of course, Claudine hadn't gotten out of bed and neither had Colton, so neither of them had yet expressed an opinion of what they wanted to do for the day. Ulla prayed they had plans that would take them out of the house. That way, she could come home and get dressed for her secret wedding with Cord without anyone suspecting what was going on.

Her prayers were answered. It seemed Colton had promised to take Claudine on a picnic with the new mayor's daughter and a friend of hers. At the store, Aunt Vida insisted Alton take her to the café for lunch and when they returned, she told Ulla she felt ready to work on her own and her niece could take the rest of the day off. "Alton will be here if I need to ask questions. Now you run along and be sure to work on your wedding, Ulla."

"I will, Aunt Vida."

And she did. That was why she was sitting in the carriage with Wilbur on the way to the church to marry a stranger. Well, not exactly a stranger, but a man she didn't really know. She wore her best dress, the yellow one Claudine had wanted. It was a voile with sprigs of ivy scattered around the skirt. The neck dipped low and the bodice fit her tiny waist perfectly. The yellow ribbons and sprigs of greenery she put in her upswept golden hair framed her face and showed off her green eyes. When she had sat back and looked at herself in the mirror in her bedroom, she couldn't help hoping Cord would like the way she looked. They would be at the church soon and she knew she'd find out how he felt then because she'd already learned she could tell a lot of what he was thinking by the look in his eyes.

"You look awfully pretty, Miss Ulla." Wilbur gave her a smile. "I'm sure your young man will be pleased to see you."

She smiled at him. "Thank you, Wilbur. I'm sorry your wife couldn't come with you to the wedding."

"She would've liked to, but she's been sick all day. I think this baby is going to give her more trouble than any of the others."

"I'm sure everything will be all right in the end and you'll have a wonderful healthy baby."

"I'm sure it will be. Doc says she's doing good and the children are lending a hand." He nodded his head. "My whole family was tickled about my new job and they said to thank you for recommending me to the banker."

"I hope you'll like the job."

"I know I will. I also know I'll be treated like a man just the way I was when I worked for your daddy."

"Oh?"

"Yep. When I went by yesterday and told Mr. Roberson that Wingate had let me go, he said I could come in today if I wanted to."

"Oh, Wilbur, I'm sorry I asked you to bring me to the church."

"Don't say that. Mr. Roberson understood. He even told me you had asked him to come see you get married and he said he'd see me at the church."

"Mr. Roberson is giving me away. You and he have been my best friends since Daddy died. I wanted you both there."

"I'm glad you're giving Pete Nettleton and his wife a chance to start a new life, too. They deserve it." He turned into the church yard. "Now, let me get close to the steps so you won't get your pretty dress dusty as you go inside."

Stuart Roberson stood at the head of the stairs with a bouquet of yellow and white flowers. He smiled broadly at her. "You look lovely, my dear. I wish your mother and father could see you."

"For some reason, I have a feeling that maybe they do."

He smiled even broader as she took Wilbur's hand to step out of the carriage. When she reached the entry, Stuart handed her the flowers.

She grinned and held the flowers to her nose to smell their wonderful fragrance. "Now I understand why you asked me what color dress I planned to get married in."

"Of course. I couldn't let you get say your vows without flowers to match your outfit. It wouldn't be right."

She leaned up and kissed his cheek and he blushed. "Has Mister ..?"

"Yes, my dear. Your Mr. Dermott is inside waiting for you. So are Mr. and Mrs. Nettleton and three fidgety children. They're all excited about this wedding."

"Then we better get started, don't you think, Papa Stuart?"

"Yes, little Ulla. That we should do."

Wilbur slipped into the church and took a seat behind the Nettletons. Mr. Roberson held his arm to her and they started down the aisle.

For a moment, Ulla wasn't sure she wasn't having a dream. The best looking man she'd ever seen stood at the altar with the preacher. He had on a black suit and his dark hair was neatly trimmed. She'd thought him handsome before, but today he topped every thought she'd ever had about him. And most important to her, his blue-gray eyes seemed to sparkle when she started toward him. Then the most brilliant smile she'd ever seen spread across his face.

~ * ~

The first time he had stepped in the general store, Cord had thought Ulla one of the prettiest women he'd ever seen, but today her real beauty shined. She looked like a mixture of a princess and an angel as she headed down the aisle to him. "Oh, Lord," he silently prayed. "Please don't let her beauty be only on the surface. I've had a wife like that and I don't think I can take another one. If Ulla turns out to be only half as decent a wife as she is beautiful, I'll be good to her and hope to love her someday. I know after what I've been through, it'll take a while, and I may never fall in love with her, but I'll try, God. I promise, I'll try."

Then she was beside him and his heart began to beat faster. He could tell she was nervous. That was all right. He figured most brides were a little jittery before their marriage.

The preacher opened his mouth to speak, but a little girl's clear voice rang out, "Is she gonna be my new mama, Daddy?"

Cord couldn't help turning to see Ivy trying to shush Becky. "Yes, honey," was all he could think of to say.

He was surprised when Ulla said, "Becky, would you like to come up here and stand with your daddy and me while we get married?"

"Yes." Becky jumped off the wooden pew and ran to them.

Cord watched as Ulla smiled at the little girl. Then she surprised him again when she said, "Why don't you go back and get Will? He should be a part of this, too."

"All right." She returned to the pew and grabbed her brother's hand. He toddled to the front of the church with his sister.

Will held out his hands to his daddy and Cord picked him up

because he didn't know anything else to do.

Ulla bent so her head was even with Becky's. "Since you're standing here with us, I'm going to make you my bridesmaid and a bridesmaid always carries flowers. Would you like to have a couple of my flowers to hold?"

Becky nodded and Ulla pulled a yellow flower and a white flower from her bouquet and handed it to the little girl.

Becky beamed and said, "We're ready now, Mr. Preacher."

Everyone smiled and the preacher cleared his throat. The couple turned back to him and said their vows. At the proper time, Cord placed the ring he'd bought in town that morning on Ulla's finger. He'd noticed the ring in the window of a store that sold a variety of jewelry and the small emerald stones in the gold band reminded him of her eyes. He hoped she'd like it and he was pretty sure she did when she glanced at him and smiled.

In a matter of minutes the preacher pronounced them man and wife. He ended the ritual with the traditional, "Mr. Dermott, you may now kiss your bride."

Cord wanted to take her in his arms and pull her close, but he guessed it was a good thing he had Will in his arms and Becky stood between them. He simply leaned over and brushed her lips with his. It shocked him at how soft her lips were and how the taste of honey seemed to slip into his mouth.

She blushed and gave him a smile, then the people in the church crowded around them offering congratulations and good wishes. Soon people began to scatter and Cord whispered to her, "Do you need to go back to town or are you ready to go out to the camp?"

"If you're ready for me, I'll go with you. I've taken care of all the business I needed to in town. I don't want to go back."

He nodded. "Pete said you'd made arrangements for someone to take you to camp."

"Yes."

Ivy walked up and Ulla said, "Ivy, Wilbur has a buggy to take you and your family to the camp unless you have other plans."

"That would be wonderful. Pete said we'd go rent something if we needed to."

Roberson walked up. "That won't be necessary. I have my buggy and I'll be happy to take anyone who doesn't have a ride out to the camp."

After a short discussion, it was decided that Wilbur would drive the Nettleton family and Stuart would take Ulla and the children. Cord said he'd ride his horse beside the buggy.

At first Will didn't want to go with Ulla, but she coaxed him and he soon gave in when he saw his sister would be there, too. Ulla couldn't help noticing how the little boy seemed to depend on Becky.

~ * ~

When they arrived at camp, they were all surprised to see that some of the emigrants had prepared a simple but lovely wedding supper for them. Naomi and Charlene met them as the buggies rolled in and started singing some song Ulla didn't recognize.

Cord dismounted and somebody offered to take care of his horse. He hurried to help Ulla and the children from the buggy. She stood close to him with Will in her arms. Becky stood in front of them.

"Aren't they a beautiful family?" Naomi shouted and a cheer went up.

"For those who haven't met her, she's Ulla," Charlene explained.

"I know her. She's the lady from the mercantile," a pretty middle-aged woman said. "My name's Beulah Reed. Me and Sam and our sons are in the wagon ahead of Cord. I'm glad to meet you again, Ulla. You sure lucked out getting to marry the most eligible bachelor on the wagon train."

"Yep," a large woman said with a chuckle. "There's gonna be some girls and women with broken hearts now that he's off the market. The girls will be upset because you got him and the women will be cross 'cause their daughters lost out and didn't get a chance at him."

"She's right. Now maybe one of my sons will have a chance for a woman." Beulah chuckled.

"What about her?" A man yelled. "I think he's a lucky man to get somebody so pretty."

"That's true," another male voice said.

"Dale's right. Take a good look at her and you'll see he's the one who had the good luck today."

"Okay, folks," Naomi said. "We'll have plenty of time to get acquainted later. Now's the time to have a party. Where's Rayburn Fields with his fiddle?"

"Pa's coming, Miss Naomi."

"Good, Judith."

Another teenager walked up to Ulla and Becky said, "This is my new mama, Kathleen."

"Hello, Kathleen. You must be Charlene's daughter," Ulla said.

Kathleen smiled. "Yes, ma'am. I thought maybe Becky would like to come sit with Esther Guggenheim and me while the grownups dance."

"Well, I..."

Ivy interrupted Ulla. "That's a good idea, Kathleen. I'm going to take little Will and watch him so Cord can dance with his new wife."

Before Ulla could protest, the party began. Raymond Fields arrived and the music started. Several people began to dance, including the bride and groom. At first Ulla felt stiff in Cord's arms, but he was an excellent dancer and she soon relaxed.

"You been dancing long, Mrs. Dermott?" he whispered in her ear.

"I can't remember the last time I danced, Mr. Dermott."

"Good. If I step on your toes, you'll probably forgive me."

She laughed. "It will probably be the other way around. As I said, it's been a long time since I danced, but I don't remember ever dancing with a man who did it as well as you."

He whirled her around and pulled her closer to him. "Just so you don't start dancing with other men so you can compare my dancing to theirs."

"I don't plan to do so."

"I appreciate that. I know the men will be asking to share dances with you, because you are awfully pretty, you know."

She stopped dancing and looked at him. "Do you really think I'm pretty?"

"Of course I do." He pulled her back in his arms. "It kind of scared me when you started down the aisle in church today."

She frowned up at him. "Why would it scare you?"

"Well, I guess it was because I thought I was marrying a woman. Then I look up and an angel is headed down the aisle toward me."

She blushed. "So you weren't disappointed in the way I looked?"

"Of course not. It was hard for me to believe you had said yes to me. I figure the man who said I was a lucky to get you was the most truthful man on this wagon train."

She blushed again. "Thank you, Cord."

"Don't mention it." He edged her away from the dancers. "Let's get something to eat. I'm hungry and I noticed they have fried chicken and it looks good. I remember how much you like it."

"I do and I think I'll try it since I'm a little hungry, too."

They made plates and moved to sit in one of the chairs from their wagon. Becky walked up. "Daddy, Miss Ivy said me and Will were going to spend the night with them. I want to, 'cause Springer is tied under their wagon and Mr. Pete said we could play with him a little before we have to go to sleep."

"That sounds like a good idea, Becky. I'm sure he's a good dog to play with."

"Joe says he won't bite me. He told me he's trained not to bark, but I heard him bark one time since we got back."

"I guess it's because of the party. He doesn't know what's going on."

"Will's done gone to sleep and I'm going to get sleepy in a little while."

"Well, honey," he started, but he knew if he didn't spend the night with his new wife the whole camp would catch on to their ruse. "I think staying with the Nettletons is a very good idea. But I think you need to give me a good night hug and one to your new mama, too."

She grinned and held her arms to him. "Good night, Daddy. I love you."

He hugged her and said, "I love you, too, Becky."

She then turned to Ulla with a grin. "Can I hug you, too?"

"I was hoping you would."

She threw her arms around Ulla's neck. "I love you, Mama. You're much better than old Miss Hilda."

Ulla smiled. "I'm glad you like me better and just so you know, I love you already, Becky."

The little girl giggled, jumped down and ran toward the Nettleton wagon.

"Thank you for telling her you love her, Ulla. I think I'm the only one who has told her that since her mother died and, like all little girls, she needs to be loved. I realize now what a huge mistake I made when I invited the Lawsons to come on this trip. She wasn't the right person to look after Becky. Besides, I have to admit, I like you better, too."

She smiled at him. "Thank you, but I wasn't just telling Becky I loved her to make her feel good. I fell in love with your little girl the day you brought her in to buy boots. The way Will clung to your head as he sat on your shoulders that day made me lose my heart to him, as well."

Cord didn't answer, but he sat his plate aside and pulled her up for another dance.

The music and the dancing went on for a while and Cord thought it had turned into a wonderful celebration. He was glad. At least if the marriage didn't work out, Ulla would have a fun night to remember. Not the wedding night he'd like to have with her, but a fun one anyway.

~ * ~

Because the wagon was to pull out the next morning, the party didn't last much longer. Ulla wanted to call the children back when it was time to settle down, but she didn't know how to do it without making all her new friends suspicious. She and Cord had agreed that nobody would ever know that their marriage wasn't one that had been planned for some time. Even the Nettletons thought they'd known each other for a little while, though she thought Ivy might suspect. Someday she might even tell her friend how the marriage really happened.

She was glad the children didn't have a problem with leaving their father. Becky had already made friends with Joe, and Will had gone to sleep soon after the festivities began, so he didn't care where he slept. Ivy had insisted on putting him in their wagon. Now, Becky was sleeping there, too.

To keep up appearances, Ulla climbed into the back of the wagon that would be their home for the next five or six months. Without a word, Cord followed her.

When they were inside, he dropped the flap, turned around to her and whispered, "I haven't forgotten my promise to you, Ulla. You don't have to worry about tonight. I'm not going to touch you."

It was good to hear him reiterate his promise and it helped her to relax somewhat. "Thank you, Cord, but I never doubted you'd not keep your word. I may not know you well, but I believe you're a man of your word."

He dropped to one of the mattresses and began taking off his boots. "What did your uncle say when you left today?"

"I didn't tell him. Aunt Vida was working in the store, so they gave me the afternoon off. It worked out perfectly for me to go home and get dressed for our wedding."

"So they didn't know you were getting married?"

"No. I was afraid they'd try to stop me. I think I told you they planned to marry me off to a dreadful man and I wanted to get away before they knew where I was going."

"I guess they'll know you've gone somewhere when you don't show up at home tonight."

"Probably not. They'll think I'm shut up in my room because I wanted to get away from them. I do that sometimes. They'll find out in the morning when I don't go downstairs to go to work in the store, but it'll be too late to do anything about it. I left them a letter wishing them well with the store and telling them Colton should marry their daughter Claudine."

"Why did you do that?"

"Because I think Claudine is going to have Colton's baby."

He lifted an eyebrow. "That doesn't bother you?"

"Not at all. I told you, to me he was a terrible man. If there was anything I could've done about it, I'd never have let them think I'd marry him in the first place. I knew all the time I couldn't stand the thoughts of being his wife. I'd rather have to spend the rest of my life alone."

"Are you saying you think I might be the better man?"

"I know you are, Cord Dermott."

"Then, I'm lucky that Colton wasn't a viable choice for you. Maybe things will work out for us quicker than you think." She didn't say anything. He chuckled and took off his coat. "I don't want to embarrass you, Ulla, so if you'll turn your back, I'm going to get out of these clothes. I've never felt comfortable in a suit like this. As soon as I'm decent, I'll provide you the same privacy to change your clothes."

Her heart beat faster as she whirled around. She didn't want to admit, even to herself, that she would have liked to watch him take his clothes off.

~ * ~

A loud horn sounded and Ulla sprang up with a little scream. She was confused and scared and not sure where she was.

"It's all right, Ulla," Cord said as he moved beside her. "It's just the wagon master blowing his trumpet. I forgot to tell you he'll be doing that at four o'clock every morning."

Still half asleep, she muttered, "Did you say four o'clock?"

"Yes. It takes a while to get the animals harnessed up and to take care of the other things that have to be done in the mornings. We have to start preparing to pull out early." Cord rose and started buttoning his pants.

"Then I better get dressed, too."

"Good idea. I don't want my new wife going out there in her night clothes."

"Don't worry, I won't." She pulled the sheet up to her chin. "What am I supposed to do while you're working with the animals?"

"Pete said last night he'd get a fire going so it would be great if you'd make us a cup of coffee. Maybe fry a little bacon. There probably won't be time for biscuits. We'll have a bigger meal later today."

"I sent some cheese and bread and a few cookies with the last things Wilbur delivered to your wagon. We can use that bread to make bacon sandwiches."

"Sounds good." He took his black hat from a peg on one of the wagon spines.

"It won't take me long to get dressed and I'll get some food together. I'll also milk the cow so the children can have milk. That's something that'll have to be done every morning, too."

He asked, "Would you check on the children as soon as they get up?"

"Yes."

"Good. I'll see you later." And he was gone.

Ulla slipped into a blue checked cotton dress, ran a comb through her hair, twisted and pinned it on the top of her head and climbed out of the wagon. She made a quick dash to the area the women used to take care of their personal needs and when she returned she heard a child whimpering. Knowing it had to be Will, she walked up to the Nettleton wagon.

Ivy turned from her position at the cook fire. "I think he wants his family."

"I'll get him. Is Becky awake?"

"Yes, I am." Becky climbed out of the wagon.

"Then you come too, honey. You can help me find your daddy some coffee."

She scrambled out of the wagon. "I know where he keeps it."

"Just bring your cups over. I already have a pot on the fire and I've started slicing the bacon. There'll be enough for all of us." She laughed. "Of course, if I remember our agreement, we're supposed to fix our meals together. We might as well start today."

"I have a loaf of bread. We can slice that to use with the bacon and as soon as I get the cow milked, we'll have milk for the children with some left over to share with others."

Will acted like he wasn't sure he wanted to go with Ulla, but when she told him they were going to find a cow, he calmed down and actually grinned.

"You go ahead and milk the cow. I'm sure the children would like a cup of milk. And I'll have the food ready when you get back. The men should be ready to eat by then, but if they're not, we'll feed the children."

"And maybe ourselves?" Ulla said with a twinkle in her eye.

"And ourselves, for sure."

"Thank you, Ivy. I'll get the bread when I get back."

"I'd like some milk with my bacon," Joe said. "I'll even go help you milk the cow if you want me to, Miss Ulla. Can Springer come?"

"Thank you, Joe, but I think you should leave Springer tied to your wagon. They're moving the oxen and other animals around and he could get hurt."

Though he looked disappointed, he said, "I'm glad you told me. I don't want Springer to get hurt."

Ulla saw his disappointment and added, "Grab one of those buckets from under my wagon and we'll get that cow milked in no time. By the time we get back, it'll probably be safe to let Springer go."

Within an hour, the cow had been milked, the milk strained, the children and the mothers all fed. Ulla sat in one of the camp chairs with Will on her lap. Becky sat in another chair beside her. They were nibbling on an apple she had peeled and sliced for them.

Joe and Springer had gone with his mother to the Mahoney wagon to take his friend, Carney and his sister, Kathleen, some milk. Ivy had returned and busied herself working around her wagon. Joe stayed at the Mahoney wagon to play with his friend, Carney.

Cord walked up leading the cow. "Well, what a pretty picture you all make."

Becky jumped up and ran to her father. "Daddy, us and Mama milked the cow and we ate bacon and now we're eating apples she made us. Miss Ivy made you some coffee, but Mama said we should drink milk."

"Milk," Will said, patted Ulla's check and giggled.

When Cord tied the cow to the back of the wagon, Ulla said, "Ivy made bacon for everyone and it's still hot and waiting for you and

Pete. I hope you don't mind that I fed the children and ate. If you'll take Will, I'll be glad to get you something."

"Don't get up. I can get it. He looks comfortable with you."

"Mama's afraid Will wants to pet the mules. He calls them cows."

Cord frowned. "Cows?"

Ulla nodded. "He keeps pointing at the mules and saying 'cow' and I'm afraid to let him down. His legs might be short, but he toddles fast when he wants to. I'm afraid he might decide he wants to pet the *cows*. Of course, now that the cow is here, he'll go straight for it, I'm sure."

"Cow." Will began to wiggle in her lap.

"Yes, sweetheart. The cow is here, but you have to stay with Mama."

"Hold him tight. We don't want him to tangle with one of the mules or the cow. They're all ornery."

"Don't worry. I will." She sighed. "I feel guilty for putting the idea in his head in the first place. I took him with me when I went to milk this morning. I held him and let him rub the cow's neck."

"Don't feel guilty, Ulla. You did nothing wrong. Kids love animals and when they're as small as Will, they have no way of knowing how dangerous it can be to make friends with a wild beast."

"I know that, but you brought me here to take care of the children and if one of them gets hurt, it'd be my fault."

"Mama won't let us get hurt, Daddy."

"Ma-ma," Will said, and patted her cheek again.

Cord smiled at his daughter. "I know she won't, Becky, and I'm not going to argue with her about it. I'm going to get some coffee and something to eat."

In a minute he was back with a cup of steaming coffee in one hand and a hunk of bread wrapped around bacon in the other. He stood beside Ulla. "It's a jumbled mess up front. Seems like every wagon is trying to get to the front of the line."

Becky stood at her father's knees. "Why don't we go first, Daddy?"

"We'll get our turn, honey. Every night when the wagons are circled, the person that was second in the row gets to be first the next day. The one that was first the previous day goes to the back of the line. We'll rotate like that daily. I figured it was best to be a ways back in the beginning. By the time we get to be first, we'll be hitting some dusty dry areas and it'll be good to be in front."

Ulla looked at him. "That makes sense. How many wagons are in the train?"

"Twenty-two."

"Then if there's an average of four people to the wagon that means we have at least eighty-eight people on this trip. A hundred and ten, if the average is five."

He chucked and winked at her. "Sounds like you still like adding things. Must be your shop-keeping background."

"I guess it does come naturally to me." She smiled at him. "If you want milk in your coffee, I set a cup in the back of the wagon and covered it with a towel. I didn't want the flies around here to get in it and there seems to be a lot of them since you hitched up the animals."

"Thank you, Ulla, but I drink my coffee black." He stood when Pete walked up.

Pete nodded. He had a cup in his hand. His voice was jovial when he said, "I see you beat me to the food."

"I did and I'm about ready for another cup of coffee. I hope you didn't drink it all."

Pete chuckled. "I made a dent in it, so you better hurry."

"I will." Cord went for more coffee.

When he returned, Pete asked. "How much longer do you think it'll be before we start moving?"

"I bet it'll be at least twenty minutes."

"I'm going to say ten."

Ivy walked up. "Those men will bet on anything. Isn't that a strange way to start a friendship?"

Ulla shook her head. "It sure is. When I'd kid my father about some silly action he pulled off with his friends, he'd laugh at me and say he was just a little boy in a grown man's skin. I'm beginning to believe all men are."

Pete turned to his wife and put his arm around her shoulder. "They don't have much faith in us, do they, Cord?"

"Doesn't sound like it."

Pete looked down at Ivy. "Where's Joe?"

"He's with his friend, Carney Mahoney. Ulla sent them some milk for breakfast. Charlene promised to send him back when they saw we were about ready to leave."

"Then he should be coming soon. I can see some wagons up ahead that look like they're starting to shift."

Becky looked at Ulla. "Joe don't want to play with me no more. He said he likes to play with boys better."

Ulla patted her arm. "Boys are like that, honey. Don't worry. When they get older, they like girls better than they do boys."

Cord shook his head. "Unfortunately that's about the time daddies don't think it's a good idea for their daughters to make friends with boys."

They all laughed.

"What's funny?"

"Nothing, Becky. Nothing." Cord patted the top of her head. "It's time I got everything in the wagon or hung on the side. We'll be moving out soon."

Ulla stood. "Then you should hang up these chairs. I'll get the milk out of the wagon so it won't spill on the mattress."

Cord took the chair and folded it. "Watch out for the cow. She's as ornery as the mules this morning."

"Cow," Will said and began patting Ulla's face for the third time. As he did, he let out a long string of jabber that nobody understood.

Seven

Vida and Alton were about half through the morning meal when he pulled out his watch. "I wonder why Ulla hasn't come down to breakfast. She usually beats me to the food."

"If she doesn't come down soon, she's going to have to work today without breakfast. I don't know if I'll allow her to leave work to get anything to eat at noon if she can't be more respectful of our rules."

"I don't blame you, Vida, but we did miss her a little after you let her go home yesterday afternoon."

"I admit you're right. She might not be good for anything else, but she sure knows everything there is to know about that store... but not to worry. We'll soon know all that she knows. She's not that smart."

He chuckled. "I guess I took it for granted she'd always be there to find whatever a customer wants. She can get to the stock room and pull it out before I can find it, but I believe you're right. With you helping, we'll be doing it soon."

"Well, don't fret while we're catching up. I have an idea what to do. I've decided that Claudine is going to start coming in to help in the store every day. She's smart and I'm sure Ulla won't mind teaching her. Before long she'll know as much about the business as our niece does." She smiled. "Then we won't need Ulla at all."

"Our plan will have worked out perfectly, won't it, my dear?"

"Yes, Alton. It sure will. Thanks to her marriage to Colton, we'll have everything we want. Then our headstrong niece will learn what it's like to have to go without everything she wants."

"I'm glad you pushed me into talking Grady into leaving the house to us without his daughter ever knowing I did it. It was the right thing to do, Vida."

"I knew we had to do it when I learned the old fool wanted to leave her everything because he said she was smart enough run the business by herself. Look where we'd be if your brother had not caved into our wishes."

"She probably could run the store, but since he put it in writing, she'll never get a chance to do it now."

Vida grinned. "That's right. Now she's turned the store over to us. All we have to do is let her teach us all about running it; then we can get rid of her."

"I thought you just said it was set that she was going to marry Colton and he was going to get the money I couldn't talk Grady into letting me manage."

"Oh I did, Alton. When we get the money, I plan to throw her and him both out of the house. I don't know what they'll do then. He's too lazy to work so I guess she'll have to support them."

"Maybe we'll give her a job in the store. I'll pay her a dollar a day, just like I do Wilbur."

"I thought you said Wilbur quit."

"That's right. He did."

"Honestly, Alton. Sometimes I think you're losing it. Do you want some more coffee?"

"A bit... then we've got to go. Maybe you better go see what's keeping Ulla."

"The lazy girl is probably trying to make us think she's sick." Vida stood. "I'll wake Claudine and have her go with us today. We might as well start implementing our plan of her learning all about the store."

Vida went up the stairs and knocked on Claudine's door. "Get up, honey. You're going to work in the store with me today."

"Oh, Mother. I don't want to get up yet."

"Don't argue with me, sweetheart. Your father and I have a wonderful plan to discuss with you. Come along, now."

"Oh, all right."

Vida moved on to Ulla's room. Knocking on the door, she yelled, "What's holding you up, girl? You're going to be late to work. Get out here."

There was no answer and Vida frowned.

She yelled again.

When there was still no answer, she tried the door. It wasn't locked and she opened it. "I'm coming in. You better be up and dressed."

Vida was shocked to see the bed made and nobody in the room. She still called out, "Ulla, where are you?"

Of course there was no answer.

Vida looked around and her eyes landed on an envelope propped against the pitcher sitting in the bowl on Ulla's dresser. She walked over and grabbed it. *Aunt Vida and Uncle Alton* was written across the front.

Vida started to rip it open, but Claudine called, "Where are you, Mama?"

"I'm here." Vida stuck the letter in her pocket and hurried to her daughter's room. "What is it, honey?"

"I'm sorry, but I'm sick, Mama. I'm throwing up and..." She grabbed her stomach and ran to the chamber pot.

"Claudine, what's the matter with you?"

"I don't know, Mama."

"Well, let me get you back to bed. I'll send your father to get the doctor."

Claudine nodded.

~ * ~

It soon looked as if the wagons would be moving and Cord walked up behind her. "Ulla, I want you and the children to start out riding in the wagon this morning."

"Why?"

"It's just a safety thing. I need to drive the team and I don't want you to have to carry Will and look after Becky at the same time."

"All right. If you insist."

Cord turned and picked up Will. After helping Ulla climb into the wagon, he handed the little boy to her, then lifted Becky inside.

Ulla sat on the mattress she'd slept on the night before.

"I can't see anything in here," Becky complained when she dropped to the other mattress.

"I'm not going to close the opening in the back. You can look out there," Cord said.

"But all I can see is Joe's wagon. It'll be coming right behind us."

Ulla smiled at her. "Don't worry, Becky. We can make do for the time being. Maybe your daddy will help me move some things around when we stop tonight and then we can open the front. You can see more then."

"You ladies work it out. I've got to get up there to drive the team. The wagon in front of us is beginning to move."

It wasn't long until their wagon jerked and began to inch forward.

Becky huffed, stuck out her lip and crossed her arms over her chest. "I still can't see nothing."

"I have a nice book in that bag over there. Why don't you get it and look at the pictures?"

"Joe's walking beside his wagon. Why can't I do that?"

"Joe's walking with his mother."

"I could walk with you."

"I know you could, honey, but if I walked, I'd have to carry Will and we wouldn't get far because he'd get heavy and I wouldn't be able to hold him."

"He can walk."

"But his legs are too short to walk fast. He couldn't keep up with you and me."

Becky's mouth twisted and Ulla was sure she was trying to think of a good argument to that last statement. She decided to stop the precocious little girl, because she was sure Becky would think of something to say. The child was smarter than most six-year-olds. "If you'll settle down and read the book, when your daddy says we can get out of the wagon, I'll see if Ivy will sit with Will and I'll walk with you and Joe. How's that?"

Becky thought a minute, twisted her mouth and wrinkled her brow. "Well, I guess it'll do, but I don't want to ride in this wagon all the way to Oregon."

Ulla reached over and hugged her. "Don't worry, sweetheart. You won't have to."

~ * ~

Vida wrung her hands and paced the hall while the doctor was with Claudine. She'd made Colton go to the store with Alton because she didn't want to leave her daughter.

The door opened and the doctor came out.

"How is she doctor? Will she be all right?"

"Don't worry, Mrs. Wingate. Your daughter is going to be fine."

"But she was awfully sick this morning."

The doctor chuckled. "That's normal."

Vida grew furious. "Normal? You must be some kind of quack. There's no way that throwing up the way Claudine was heaving this morning can be normal."

"Calm down, Mrs. Wingate. Yes, throwing up the way your daughter was doing is perfectly normal when a woman is with child."

"What?"

"Your daughter is pregnant, Mrs. Wingate. I'd say she's about two and a half to three months along."

"No!" Vida grabbed her face. "You have to be wrong."

"I'm not wrong, ma'am."

"But she's not married."

"Then, Mrs. Wingate, I suggest you find the man who is responsible and make sure she's married soon or else your daughter will be marked for life. Unfortunately that happens to women who have a child out of wedlock."

"Oh, my lord, this can't be happening to me." She turned to the doctor and demanded. "Who is the father?"

"I have no idea. I think you need to discuss that with your daughter."

"But I've told my daughter not to be with a man until she's married. I wanted her to be a virgin, not give her husband used merchandise."

"Again, that's between you and your daughter, ma'am." He nodded at Vida. "I've done all I can here so I'll show myself out."

Vida ignored him and headed into Claudine's room.

~ * ~

It was noon when the wagon train came to a stop.

"I don't want to stop, Mama," Becky said. "You and me haven't been walking beside the wagon long enough."

"You daddy told me that we'll always stop at noon so the mules and oxen and other livestock could rest and be watered. See, he's climbing down from the wagon. Let's go speak to him."

"I don't want to stop yet, Daddy."

"Can't be helped, honey. We'll be nooning here."

She frowned. "What's nooning?"

"It's the middle of the day when we stop to water and rest the animals and get ourselves a bite to eat. We'll all rest a while, too."

"I'm not tired."

"If you don't want to rest, you can play. Now, why don't you and your mama go fix us a something to eat? I've got to take care of the cow and the mules."

"Oh, all right." She stomped away.

Cord shook his head. "Our first day out and she's bored already."

"Don't worry. She'll soon get used to the routine." She smiled at him. "I'll get the chairs unfolded and fix the food."

"Thank you." He turned to the team.

Ulla went to the wagon, climbed in and got the basket of food she'd sent out to the wagon train earlier. There was plenty for the noon meal.

Ivy came up with Will in her arms. "He just woke up."

Ulla handed her the basket. "Do you mind setting this out? I'm sure there's enough for all of us."

"From the looks of what you've packed, I'm sure there will be. I've got some pickles and some canned peaches we can add if you want to."

"That sounds great."

"Is Becky...?"

"Don't worry. She and Joe are playing with Springer. I told him he had to stay with us during this break. He grumbled a little, but finally said he guessed it wouldn't be too bad to spend it playing with Becky."

Ulla chuckled and put Will on the mattress. "Boy, you're wet. I hope I can get you trained to go to the weeds soon. I'm going to have a mountain of diapers to wash whenever we get near a river or lake or something."

Will giggled.

"Just like a man, Ulla," Ivy said. "They mature at their own pace. Of course, some of them never grow up. They just giggle at us and steal our hearts."

"So true." She nuzzled Will's cheek. "This little fellow sure has stolen mine."

"You're a good mama to the children, Ulla."

"I'm trying to be, Ivy. I love them and I want them to love me."

"You don't have to worry. All three of the Dermotts already do." She turned. "I better get the food ready. I'm sure the men will want to eat as soon as they can."

"All we have to do is make them coffee and they'll be happy."

"That's for sure."

Ulla turned her attention back to Will. "Sweetie, you sure have a crazy looking birthmark on your little hiney."

He giggled and waved his arms.

"Yes, my little love. I know you don't care, but I think it makes you unique."

"Ma'ma." He reached for her.

"Yes, Will. I'm your mama now and I'm a lucky woman to get a fine son like you."

Will only giggled again.

~ * ~

At two o'clock, it was time to start the wagons moving again. Cord said, "I think we can all walk for a while."

"Who'll guide the team?"

"I think I can guide them with my whip."

"I look forward to being out of the wagon for a while, but I doubt I can carry Will very far without tiring."

"Don't worry. I'll carry him." He hoisted Will to his shoulders.

"I'm big, I'll walk." Becky looked up at her daddy. "Can I carry the whip?"

"No, honey. I'll carry the whip. I'll walk next to the wagon and you walk on the other side of your mama."

"Why can't I walk beside you?"

"Because if I have to do something to control the team, I'll need to hand Will to Ulla in a hurry. She should be beside me just in case."

"Hey, Becky," Joe came running up. "Ma said you and me could play with Springer if we'd stay between her and your folks. Want to?"

"Sure." She looked up at Ulla. "Can I, Mama?"

"You can if your father thinks it's safe."

He nodded. "Go ahead, honey. Just do like Miss Ivy said. Stay where you can be seen."

She skipped off with her friend and his dog.

"Ulla, I don't want you to think you always have to ask me when Becky wants to do something. You're her mama now and you have a say so in what she does."

"I didn't want you to think I was trying to take over your children."

"I don't think that. From what I see, Becky already thinks of you as her mother. Didn't she just ask you for permission to play with Joe and I was right here? If she thought she should, she'd have asked me."

"She did do that."

"That's the way I want it to be. I'll back you on your decisions about her and I hope you'll back mine."

"Of course, I will, Cord." She smiled up at him. "I assume you mean the same goes for Will."

"Sure," was all he said.

Ulla wondered why he didn't say more, but she didn't ask.

"Walk," Will said, and started patting Cord's head.

"No, Will."

"Walk." He looked at Ulla.

Cord's voice grew angry. "I said, no, Will."

Will sniffed and began to cry.

Ulla saw Cord bite his lip and wondered what he was going to do, but she didn't say anything. She didn't see it was her place to tell him how to react to his children.

The little boy reached out his arms. Through tears he blubbered, "Mama."

Cord took him off his shoulders. He turned and handed Will to Ulla. "You take him for a little while. I need to check the team, then I'll carry him again."

Ulla didn't see that anything had changed with the team, but she took Will without saying anything to Cord. She did look at Will and whisper, "I've got you, sweetheart. Now, stop crying if you can."

After they walked for a little while, Will patted her chest. "Walk."

"If I let you walk a little, you must hold to Mama's hand."

"Hand."

She sat him on the ground. "Now take my hand."

Will put his chubby little hand in hers and grinned. "Me walk."

"Yes, my little love. You're walking."

Cord didn't return to them and she watched as his long strides kept pace with the mules. She wondered what had happened to make him act the way he did with Will. She hoped it wasn't something she did or said.

It wasn't long until Becky and Joe passed them. "I told you Will could walk, Mama."

"He's doing a fine job. He's just a little slow."

"I know." She turned back to Joe and said, "Do you think Springer likes me?"

"I don't know. He's a dog."

"Well, if he didn't like me, he'd bite me, wouldn't he?"

Ulla didn't hear Joe's answer because they were far enough ahead that the wagons drowned out their conversation.

Ivy came up beside her. "I see you have a new escort."

"I do. Isn't he handsome?"

"Very handsome, but I'm afraid he's going to walk so slow that you'll be at the back of the line of wagons in a few minutes."

"That wouldn't surprise me at all. I plan to let him walk a little longer, then I'll carry him a while."

"I'll help you."

"Thank you, Ivy."

A little later, Ulla said, "I'm getting tired and I know you are, too."

"Maybe a little."

"I'm going to see if I can catch up with Cord and let him put us in the wagon. Thank you for your help with Will, Ivy."

"It was my pleasure. I'll see you when we stop for the evening. Cord told Pete he thought you might make biscuits for us."

Ulla smiled. "I plan to and I hope you're not disappointed."

"Oh, I'm sure none of us will be."

"I'll get Joe to help you." She called her son.

He and Becky ran up. "Yea, Ma."

"Miss Ulla wants to get in her wagon. Run up ahead and tell Mr. Cord she's coming and wants him to help her and Will get inside."

"Yes, ma'am." He ran off.

"Are you tired, Mama?"

"A little bit, Becky." She looked into the little girl's eyes. "How about you?"

"I'm not tired, but if you want me to get in the wagon and help you with Will, I will."

"That might be a good idea. I might go to sleep and let him fall out."

"If you go to sleep, I won't let him." She grinned. "I'll go tell Daddy."

Ulla scooped Will closer and hurried her pace when she saw Cord turn and head toward her. She couldn't help remembering how short Cord had been with Will earlier. She didn't want to give him an excuse to snap at the boy again.

When they met, Cord said, "Joe said you and Will wanted to ride in the wagon."

"I want to ride, too, Daddy."

He nodded and took Will. He put the boy on his shoulders. "Now, let me pick you up, Becky. I'm going to sit you in the wagon, but we have to hurry. I don't want Pete's team to run over us."

She reached up her arms to him. "All right, Daddy."

"Ulla, you stay from behind the wagon until I get the children in, then I'll help you."

She nodded and watched as he swung Becky over the tailgate. "Scoot back, honey. I'm going to put Will in and you tell him to crawl to you."

She heard Becky say, "I will, Daddy."

"Daddy," Will said and giggled.

Cord ignored him and sat him over the tailgate.

Ulla heard Becky say, "Come here, Will. Come to Becky."

Cord turned to Ulla. "You ready?"

"If you'll help me step up on the tailgate, I think I can get in by myself."

He nodded, but when he took her by the waist, he simply lifted her over the barrier and winked. "Didn't want you to fall."

She blushed. "I'm glad you didn't let me fall. It would have been embarrassing."

"As well as dangerous. I don't want you to get hurt. If you did, I'd miss out on the biscuits you're going to make tonight." He winked at her again and walked off before she could say anything more.

Eight

Vida met Alton and Colton at the door when they came in from the store shortly after six-thirty. "We didn't have much business today," Alton explained. "That wagon train pulled out this morning. I was hungry and I didn't see any reason to stay open until seven as usual."

Vida didn't say anything about him closing the store early or about anything to eat. "Both of you have a seat. We have something to talk about."

"What is it, Vida? Can't we talk over the supper table?"

"I said come in the parlor and set down. Now do it and don't argue with me."

"I don't understand."

She glared at him. "I said, don't argue."

"Come on, Alton, let's get this over with," Colton said"

They entered the parlor behind Vida and saw Claudine sitting on the divan. She looked drawn and pensive and anyone could tell she'd been crying. Colton joined her and whispered, "Are you all right?"

Claudine didn't answer and Alton took the chair facing them without speaking. Vida sat in the chair beside him.

Alton broke the silence. "Well, it looks like you have something serious to discuss, Vida. What in the world is going on?"

"It's not only serious, Alton, but it's something we have to take care of immediately." Vida glared at Colton when she added, "That sorry-good-for-nothing distant cousin of mine has gone and made our sweet innocent daughter pregnant with his child."

Alton looked stunned. "No. It can't be true. You have to be mistaken."

"No, I'm not mistaken. The doctor said the sickness she had this morning was because of her condition."

"I don't believe it."

"Well, husband..."

Colton's voice broke in. "Is she right, Claudine? Are you going to have a baby?"

"Yes, Colton." She looked at him and gave him a weak smile. "I'm going to have your baby."

He looked scared. "How can I be sure it's my child?"

"Of course it's your child. You're the only man I've ever been with."

"I don't know if I believe you." He stood. "Cousin Vida says I'm going to marry Ulla and get her money and..."

Vida stood. Her eyes peered into his and she pointed a finger at him. "Sit down, Colton. Things have changed. You're not marrying Ulla. You're marrying Claudine and you're marrying her tonight."

"Now wait a minute...."

Alton stood and shoved him back on the divan. "You scum. If Vida says you've gotten our daughter in a family way, you did. Furthermore, you will marry her. I'll not have her disgraced."

"Colton," Claudine almost screamed. "You said you loved me."

"I...I..."

Alton glared at him. "Shut-up, Colton. You have no say in this matter."

"But what about Ulla's money."

"I'll think of another way to get Ulla's money and I don't need your help to do it." Vida sneered at him.

Alton turned to Vida, "By the way, where is Ulla? She'll overhear us if we're not careful."

"I don't know where she is. I figured she went on to work before we got up."

"She never showed up at the store today."

Vida shook her head. "That sorry good-for-nothing. She is sure trying my patience, but I'll deal with her later." She looked back at Colton. "There's no need to fight me any longer. The wedding will take place tonight."

He looked as if he wanted to say something, but he only nodded.

"Now that's settled. Let's eat, then handle this situation as soon as possible tonight."

They stood and trooped into the dining room.

"When they were half way through the meal, Claudine looked at her mother. "Should we invite Ulla to the wedding?"

Her father looked at her. "If she's not here, how can we?"

"I wonder where she could be?"

It was as if a sudden realization fell on Vida. "With all that's going on, I completely forgot that I went into her room this morning. I found it empty, but she left a note." Vida took it out of her pocket. "I was so upset with Claudine today, I didn't read it. Maybe I should read it now."

"Read it aloud, dear. We're all curious."

She nodded, ripped the letter open and began to read.

Dear Aunt Vida and Uncle Alton. When you get this letter, you will know that I'm gone. Since I have turned the store over to you, I can't help giving you some advice in hopes that it will help you. First of all, you need to be careful as to how you run the business. I know your heart is not in Wingate's General Store, but if you don't take more of an interest, it will fail and you will be out of a way to make a living. Claudine is terrible at ordering and the stock is so low now that there won't be nearly enough to supply the wagon train that will leave in a few weeks. Without Wilbur's help, I'm afraid you won't be able to handle things unless you work hard and find a way to replenish the supplies you will need to fill the orders. I'm only telling you this to let you know that if the store fails, unless you have the money yourself, there is nothing else to help you build it back up. I have made arrangements for my money to be transferred to the bank where I'll be settling, so please do not think you can count on that to ease your financial woes."

Vida looked up and her eyes showed her anger. "The nerve of her!"

"I agree, Vida," Alton said, "but continue. She must tell us more than this."

Vida raised an eyebrow, but she did continue.

As for me, I have met a widowed man with two children and he has asked me to marry him. I don't love Colton and don't want to marry him, so I have decided to marry this man and move away with him. I feel this is the best thing for all of us.

On another note, I know Colton and Claudine are in love and she is the one he should marry—and marry soon before something happens between them that they can't change and will cause the family a lot of embarrassment.

Good luck to all of you.

Your niece, Ulla Wingate

"Do you mean we can't get her money?" Alton said.

"That's what the bitch says." Vida's mouth twisted into an ugly sneer.

Alton put his fork down. "I'm going to talk to the bank about that. It don't seem right."

"For heaven's sake, Alton." Colton jumped up. "She's thrown me over for some bum with two children. I bet he only married her for that money. Money I was looking forward to and money that would help me leave this dump of a town forever."

"You were going to leave me?" Claudine reached out and hit him in the side.

"Well, no." He looked sheepish. "You could come with me."

"Nobody's going anywhere!" Vida shouted. She looked at the letter one more time. "When we came here I thought it would be easy to outsmart this little bitch, but it looks like it's the other way around."

"Maybe we can stop the marriage," Alton suggested."

Vida shook her head. "How?"

"Well, we could say she's touched in the head."

"Don't be a fool. Do you think anybody in this town would believe us? She's done business with them for years and they'd come to her defense in an instant."

Alton looked lost. "Then what are we going to do, Vida?"

"The first thing we're going to do is get Claudine and Colton to the preacher so they can get married tonight. After that's taken care of, I suggest we go to the store and see what we can do about trying to save the business. Now finish eating and let's get this night over with."

They all looked at her, but nobody argued. Seldom did anyone argue with Vida.

~ * ~

The sun in the west hung low enough to leave the sky streaked in bright colors of red and gold with touches of purple. The wagons had circled where the scout had indicated they'd camp for the night. By the time the animals were unhitched, watered and fed and put in the corral formed by circling the wagons, the fire was blazing under the vegetable stew Ivy was stirring. Ulla had the biscuits in the Dutch oven ready to bury in the coals for baking.

Pete and Cord walked up and took two of the chairs hanging on the side of the wagon and set them beside the two already set up near where Joe and Becky were playing a game they'd carved in the dirt. Will sat on the ground near his sister.

He looked up and saw Cord. "Daddy."

Cord looked at the little boy. "Yes, Will."

Becky butted in. "Daddy, will you watch him? Joe and me want to go play with Springer."

"Why don't you bring Springer over here?" Cord asked.

Joe said, "Ma said we couldn't bring him over here where the food is. I don't know why."

Pete grinned at them. "Go ahead and play with Springer, kids. Your pa and I'll watch him while we attend to business."

Becky and Joe ran to the Nettleton wagon and Ulla stood from burying her biscuits in the coals. "So you have business." She walked over and took the vacant chair beside Cord.

"Mama!" Will cried. He left his daddy's knees and ran to her with his hands held up. "Take."

Ulla picked him up. "Sweetie, you sure are dirty. I'll have to give you a quick wash before we eat."

"Eat."

"We'll eat in a little while."

He snuggled against her and nodded. She knew it was because he was sleepy, not because he agreed to what she'd said and was satisfied.

"All right, fellows," Ivy sat beside her husband. "What's this business you two have to handle?"

"It's simple, honey. Cord and I decided we'd have something to bet on each day on this trip. One will choose what the bet will be in the morning and we'll settle it in the evening."

"Why in the world would you do that?"

"We thought it would keep us busy thinking up items to bet on. It will also give us something special to look forward to each night."

Ulla looked at Cord. "What's this big bet going to cost us if you lose every night?"

"Nothing big." Cord reached over and patted her knee. "We plan to have a cigar after supper each night. The loser supplies the cigar."

Ulla laughed. "Well, thank goodness, you won't be spending all the family money gambling."

"I agree," Ivy said. "Now, what did you bet on today?"

"And who chose it?" Ulla asked.

"We bet on how long it would take our wagon to start rolling after the first one took off. Cord chose."

"I said it'd take twenty minutes and Pete said it'd take ten. It actually took fifteen."

Ivy turned her head. "So, for your first bet, it was even. I guess that means you'll each supply your own cigars tonight."

"That's right." Cord turned to Ulla. "See, I didn't lose a dime of our family fortune."

"I'm glad of that." She stood and plopped Will in his lap. "I think it's time to get the biscuits out of the fire."

"Great, I'm starving." Pete looked at Ivy. "Your stew smells good, too, sweetheart."

She chuckled. "Thanks, dear."

Ulla uncovered the Dutch oven and removed the biscuits. She hoped everyone would like them. Especially Cord. Glancing at him, she almost frowned. He looked so stiff and uncomfortable with Will on his lap and she couldn't help wondering why. He was often happy and playful with Becky, but so different with Will. This was something she was going to investigate. A father shouldn't make a difference between his children. And knowing Cord was a fair and gentle man, it went against his character to be this way with Will. There had to be a reason and she wouldn't rest until she found out what it was.

~ * ~

Three days after leaving Independence, Ulla sat on the wagon seat with Becky between her and Cord. Will was in her lap asleep. "Cord, I've been noticing that mountain in the distance. It looks strange and out of place here on the prairie."

He nodded. "Mr. Pruitt said it's called Blue Mound, but nobody knows why it cropped up out here. We'll probably pause for a while for a rest when we get closer. He said some people like to climb it, but soon see that there's nothing but prairie on the other side."

"Can I climb upon top of it, Daddy?"

"I think not, Becky. We'll just take advantage of the time to rest."

She looked at Ulla. "Will you climb it with me, Mama?"

Ulla shook her head. "No, Becky. Daddy said no to your climbing it and I agree with him. We need to rest."

Becky huffed and crossed her arms across her chest as she often did when she didn't get her way, but she didn't say anything else.

Cord looked across the top of her head and winked at Ulla.

She knew he was thanking her for backing him up on his decision to keep Becky off the hill. She gave him a slight nod and smiled. She decided to change the subject and see if Becky would join the conversation. "Ivy asked me to make biscuits again tonight. I hope you'll enjoy them again."

He nodded. "I sure will. Your biscuits were great. I think I could handle them every night. How about you, Becky. Do you like Mama's biscuits?"

She nodded, but didn't answer.

"How far do you suppose we've come, Cord?"

"Mr. Pruitt said we'd probably average fifteen or sixteen miles a day. Could even make twenty on a good day." He laughed and added, "Since we've been gone three days and haven't had any trouble so far, that'll be about fifty miles or so."

Ulla laughed, too. "You read my mind. I was about ready to figure it in my head."

"I guessed that."

Before she could answer, a piercing scream filtered to them. It was followed by several other screams as the wagons began to slow down and come to a halt.

Becky grabbed her father's arm. "Who was that?"

Cord was pulling back on the reins, stopping the mules and didn't answer.

Ulla reached over and patted her arm. "We'll find out in a minute, sweetheart. I just hope nobody's hurt."

Becky turned to her and snuggled close. "Me, too."

Ulla put her arm around Becky. "Why don't we say a prayer that whatever happened won't be a bad thing?"

Will began to wake up and wiggled in Ulla's lap. She pulled him close to her chest. "It's fine, sweetheart."

He grinned and looked at Becky.

She reached over and squeezed his leg. "We'll be fine, Will. Mama will take care of us while Daddy is busy."

Mr. Pruitt rode beside the wagons waving his hat, giving them the motion to stop as quickly as they could. Ulla would have liked to ask him what was going on, but she knew it wasn't the time. She'd have to be patient.

Cord set the brake on the wagon and glanced at her. "Stay in the wagon with the children and I'll see what I can find out."

She nodded.

"Can I go with Daddy?'

"No, Becky. It could be dangerous. You have to wait here with Will and me."

She turned to her father, who was climbing out of the wagon. "I want to go with you, Daddy."

Cord glanced at Ulla, paused and shook his head. "Becky, there's no need to ask me if I'll let you come when your mama has said you must stay here. Listen to her and I'll be back soon."

Ulla wanted to smile, but she wouldn't let herself. Cord had backed her the way she did him. This was going to work. Soon Becky would learn she couldn't pit one parent against the other, trying to get her way.

The air on the prairie was still and hot. Ulla would have liked to climb down from the wagon, but after refusing to let Becky, she knew she had to sit still, too.

Becky looked up at her. "What happened, Mama?"

"I don't know, honey. Maybe your daddy will be back soon and he can tell us."

"I hope so. I'm hot."

"Me, too."

"Why don't we get down?"

Ulla shook her head. "We need to wait here. I'm sure your father will be back soon."

"When will he get here?"

"Soon, but ... Oh, I see him coming now."

When Cord reached them, the somber man climbed back to the wagon seat. "There was an accident. Mr. Pruitt said we were going to go ahead and stop here for the day because by the time Dr. Guggenheim gets through with the patient, it'll be time to stop anyway."

"Maybe we can still climb that mountain there." Becky's voice was hopeful.

He shook his head. "No, Becky. We all have to stay near the wagon today."

"I bet Kathleen would climb the mountain with me. Can I go see?"

"Not today."

Becky turned toward Ulla and started to say something, but changed her mind when Ulla shook her head. Becky crossed her hands on her chest and didn't say anything more.

Ulla figured it was because she could tell her father was upset and didn't want to push the idea of climbing the mountain any further. She turned to Cord and asked in a calm voice, "What happened, Cord?"

"The Kingston boy decided to climb off the wagon while it was moving. He got his foot caught and fell."

Though his actions told her he didn't want to talk about it, she couldn't stop herself from asking, "Is he hurt badly?"

"The wagon ran over his leg."

Ulla put her hand to her cheek. "Oh no. Is it broken?"

"Worse." He gave her a look that said he didn't want to say anything more in front of Becky.

Ulla nodded and muttered, "I'm sorry."

After circling the wagons, Cord took Will then helped Ulla and Becky to the ground. Handing Will back to Ulla he said, "Stay close to the wagon while I take care of the animals. I won't be long."

She nodded. "Come along, Becky. I need to dry Will and you can help me."

"Mama," Becky said as she handed Ulla a diaper, "why is Daddy mad?"

"Oh, sweetie, your father isn't mad. He's just upset."

"Why?"

"I suppose it's because he saw how badly the Kingston boy was hurt."

"I don't understand."

Ulla took a deep breath and wondered what words she should use to satisfy Becky's curiosity. "I guess it's because he was thinking how terrible it would be if you or Will had an accident and was hurt."

Becky looked up at Ulla. "He'd rather Will got hurt than me."

Ulla was shocked, but tried not to show it. "Why in world would you say such thing, Becky? I'm sure your father loves you both very much."

Becky shook her head. Her voice was matter of fact when she said, "He loves me a whole lot more than he loves Will."

~ * ~

Cord stopped cold when he heard his daughter's declaration. He'd staked the cow outside of the ring so she could graze until time to milk her this evening. He then decided to return to tell Ulla not to talk about the accident to Becky until he got back from unhitching the mules and taking them down to the corral made by the circled wagons. He felt it was his place to impress on her how dangerous this trip could be if children didn't obey their parents and he wanted to do it in a way that wouldn't scare his child.

Now he waited to see what Ulla would say to Becky's declaration.

Ulla's voice was soft and gentle when she said, "I have no doubt that your father loves you very much. Who wouldn't love a sweet little girl like you? Why, I've only been your mother for a few days and I love you already."

"Do you love me better than Will?"

"Can I tell you a secret, Becky?"

Cord's heart seemed to skip. Was Ulla actually going to admit to loving Becky more that Will or was it the other way around?

"Yes, Mama."

"This is a secret that a mama and a daddy never let their children know. It has been around since Adam and Eve had their sons."

"What is it?"

"Mamas and daddies have a secret way of letting each one of their children think that they love them more than any of their other brothers and sisters in the family. It doesn't matter if there are only two children, like there is in your family, or if the family consists of a dozen children. That's why you think your daddy loves you better than he does Will. When Will gets older, I'm sure he'll think his daddy loves him the best."

Cord could almost see Becky thinking over what Ulla was saying. So was he. He'd known form the beginning that the woman was smart, but until this moment, he hadn't realized how smart. Of course, he knew he loved Becky more, but he couldn't help it. There was no doubt that Becky was his child and there was a lot of doubt about Will. No man could love another man's offspring as much as he loved his own. But how about a woman?

It then dawned on him that Ulla hadn't given birth to either of these children, yet she did seem to love them both. And love them equally. Would this be true if she had a child of her own?

Becky's voice interrupted his thoughts. "You love me, don't you?"

"Oh, Becky. Come here and let me hug you. I don't want you to ever think I don't love you because if you think that, you're very wrong. I love you with all my heart. It doesn't matter if your father and I have a bunch of other children someday, you'll always be my special daughter."

"I love you, too, Mama. Do I have to love you more than I love Daddy?"

"No, Becky. Don't ever let such a thought into your head. You should never have to choose between your father and me because we both love you. I know I'm your new mother and it makes me happy that you love me already. Just love us both and that will always make me happy and I'm sure it will make your daddy happy, too."

She was right. It did make him happy. Moving quietly, he decided he'd not interrupt them. He walked to the front of the wagon to unhitch the mules. He knew he shouldn't have eavesdropped on the conversation, but he couldn't help being glad he did. Though they still had to consummate the marriage, from what Ulla had said, he knew that she did plan to have children with him someday. In spite of the sadness that had hit the train, he couldn't help feeling a little happy, knowing she would be his in the future instead of him only hoping this to be so.

Nine

Charlene Mahoney and her son walked up while Ulla had her hands in the big wooden bowl making biscuit dough. Ivy was stirring the stew in the big pot hanging over the fire. "Hello, ladies," she greeted them.

"Hello, Charlene." Ulla looked up. She could tell from the woman's look that she had something on her mind. "Would you like a cup of coffee?"

"I just made a fresh pot," Ivy said. "The men said they'd want some when they got back."

"No, thank you. I just came back to your wagon with Carney. He said he wanted to play with Joe and I thought I'd visit with you and Ivy for a tad."

From Charlene's well-chosen words, Ulla knew that she didn't want Carney coming alone to their wagon and used visiting them as an excuse to come with him. She knew she'd have done the same thing if it had been Becky.

"You can look over there and see that Joe and Becky are under our wagon playing with Springer," Ivy said. "Why don't you go join them, Carney?"

His face lit up. "Can I, Mama?"

"Of course."

As soon as he moved to the Nettleton wagon, Charlene added, "Where's the baby?"

"Will couldn't stay awake any longer. He's taking a nap in that tent beside the wagon. I didn't put him inside because I was afraid he'd try to climb out when my back was turned. I have the tent in my view all the time." Ulla smiled at her.

"I'm sorry, Ulla. I know you wouldn't let him out of your sight. I guess I'm just jittery because I was there when the Kingston boy fell from the wagon. It's left me pretty upset."

"I'm sure." Ivy smiled at her. "As soon as Ulla gets those biscuits in the Dutch oven, why don't I make us a cup of tea instead of the coffee? I could use one and I bet you and Ulla could, too."

"I sure would. We have no idea how long the men will be gone, so we might as well relax while we can." Ulla began wadding up rounds of dough and placing them in the Dutch oven.

"I do think it was smart of them to decide to go on a hunting excursion since we had to stop so early today. I hope they bring back a deer or at least a turkey or two. It would taste good."

After the biscuits were under the coals and the tea was made, the three women sat so all the children were in their sights. Ulla broke the silence. "I'm sure it was a shock to see the Kingston child hurt, Charlene. Could you tell us what happened?"

"I was walking with Mrs. Kingston and we were slightly behind her two children. I'm not sure what made him do it, but his sister said he was taunting her and saying he could ride on the rim of the tailgate without falling off. She said she told him he better not because his mother would get mad. He laughed and went running up behind the wagon and tried to pull himself up, but he couldn't get a tight hold and he was slung to the side. His left leg was caught under the wagon wheel and it was practically cut off."

"Oh my!" Ivy gasped. "Do you think the doctor will be able to save the leg?"

Charlene shook her head. "All the bones in the leg were not only broken, but most of the flesh was severed and there was nothing the doctor could do but finish amputating it."

"That is so tragic." Ulla took a deep breath. "Cord and Pete told us it was bad, but I guess they didn't want to tell us how bad until everything was certain."

"Probably. Liam said he wished he could have shielded me from it, but there was no way since I was right there."

"How old is the Kingston boy?"

"He's twelve, Ivy. Much too old to try something so foolish, but sometimes I wonder if the male of the species ever grows up."

"You're right. I think it was great of Mr. Pruitt to insist some of the men leave the train and hunt while we're camped. Cord took him up on it right away. Of course, before he left he gave me all kinds of instructions about watching the children." She shook her head. "I don't think most men know how protective a woman can be over her sons and daughters."

"Pete did the same thing."

Charlene chuckled. "So did Liam, and that man has never been hunting more than a half dozen times in his life. We lived in Chicago. He's been a lawyer all his career and he's never known anything about such things as hunting."

Ivy frowned. "I'm surprised you decided to come on this trip."

Charlene gave her a half smile. "Things didn't go well in Chicago and Liam said we needed to come to a new part of the country and start a new life." She offered no more explanation.

Ulla didn't want to ask because she sensed it was something Charlene didn't want to talk about. She changed the subject. "Do you have any idea how much longer it'll be before we move on?"

"Naomi told me the Kingstons have decided they'll return to Independence. It seems they don't have the heart to go on with the train. Besides, they think their son can get better medical care there."

Ivy shuddered. "I can understand that. If it were Joe, I wouldn't want to go on either."

Ulla frowned. "Is the boy able to stand the trip back to Independence?"

"Saul said he could probably stand it better than going forward. The first of the trail is the easiest part. It gets rougher the closer to the mountains we get. Of course that'll be a while yet."

"Mama!" Becky came running up.

"What's the matter, Becky?"

She came to Ulla's side. Sobbing, she managed to say, "Joe and Carney are going to slip off and they won't let me go."

Ivy came to her feet. "We'll just see about that." She headed to her wagon with Charlene on her heels.

Becky's eyes got big. "I didn't mean to get them in trouble."

"You did the right thing, honey." A whimper came from the tent beside the wagon. "Sounds like your brother is waking up."

"I didn't mean to wake him up."

"That's fine, honey. It's time he got up anyway." She stood and took Becky's hand. "Want to help me get him up?"

"I want to go with Carney and Joe."

"Don't worry about that. I'm sure Joe and Carney won't be going anywhere. Their mothers will see to that."

Ulla was right. The boys didn't go anywhere.

~ * ~

After the Dermotts went to bed in the wagon, it didn't take the children long to go asleep. Will was cuddled against Ulla and Becky was between him and her father. Ulla was having a hard time going to sleep and she wondered if Cord was also. Though his back was turned to them, his breathing hadn't become slow and steady as it usually did. The nights he'd spent in the wagon, Ulla had always known when he drifted off.

Wondering why he was having trouble tonight, she whispered, "Can't you sleep, Cord?"

"Sorry if I'm keeping you awake."

"You're not. I can't get that Kingston boy off my mind."

He turned over. "It was a horrible thing for all of us, but especially for his parents."

"Charlene Maloney told Ivy and me they've decided to go back to Independence."

"They did. Saul Guggenheim went with them to make sure the boy is cared for on the trip back to town."

"I understand, but I hate to see them go. Naomi is such a good friend."

"Naomi and their boys didn't go, because Saul's not going to stay in town. Their daughter did go with them because he needed the help and didn't think Mrs. Kingston could hold up to do it. He and Esther plan to return to the train as soon as he sees the boy is taken care of."

"But won't we be so far from town?"

"You're right, if you're talking about a wagon, Ulla, but they are going to come back on horses. It won't take them that long to catch up with us. I even offered him my horse for one of them to ride back and they took me up on it."

"That was nice of you, Cord."

"I wasn't just being nice. I wanted Saul to come back and travel with us. Besides liking the man, I thought it was a good idea to have a doctor on this train."

"You're right about that."

There was a moment of silence, then Cord whispered, "Can I ask you something, Ulla?"

"Of course."

"Do you really believe in love?"

She was stunned by his question, but she knew she had to respond. "Of course I do. Don't you?"

"I believe in certain kinds of love."

"For instance?"

"I believe in a love between a parent and a child. I also believe in love between brothers."

When he said nothing more, she asked, "What about love between a husband and a wife?"

"I can't name a couple who I ever met who really loved each other."

Ulla's heart fell to her stomach. Did this mean there was no hope of him ever falling in love with her even though she realized she was beginning to fall for him? She took a deep breath. "You're wrong, Cord Dermott. I know for a fact that my mother and father were very much in love with each other. They showed it in the way they reacted to each other and to others."

"Maybe they kept their real feelings hidden from you. Parents tend to do that to spare their children's feelings. I know mind did. Oh, they cared for each other, but about deep abiding love between them wasn't something I thought they had."

Ulla was ready to argue with him when Becky stirred. She kind of sat up and muttered, "What are you saying to me?"

Ulla reached over Will and patted her. "It's nothing, sweetheart. Go back to sleep. There won't be any more talking."

Becky settled down and Cord said nothing further. Neither did Ulla, though she wasn't sure when either of them went to sleep.

~ * ~

Nothing was said about the conversation the next day, but Ulla had it on her mind. She tried her best to act as if nothing had happened, though she noticed Cord was quieter than usual. She decided the best thing she could do was try not to let him see how hurt she'd been by his ideas about love.

When they stopped for the nooning, she and Ivy decided to roast some of the meat from the deer the men had killed and dressed the day before. Everyone in the camp seemed to be doing the same. Nobody wanted the meat to go to waste. They knew they could dry some of it or cure it by covering it in salt, but mostly it needed to be cooked and eaten in the next couple of days.

When the men returned from settling the animals, they were ready to eat. Pete said, "I sure hope your wife made some of her biscuits to eat with this, Cord."

"I know you do because you bet she would make them."

Ivy laughed. "You men sure find the craziest things to bet on."

When Ulla said nothing, Cord chuckled. "I assure you there's nothing crazy about my wife's biscuits."

"I didn't mean to imply there was." Ivy looked contrite.

"Don't worry, Ivy. I know you didn't," Ulla said. "I agree with you. They do bet on crazy things and my making biscuits doesn't seem strange when you consider the other bets they've made."

"Well," Pete looked at them. "Are you going to tell us what we're going to eat with our meat?"

"No." Ivy shook her head. "You're going to have to wait and see."

They did have biscuits and Pete said he was going to enjoy the cigar Cord would supply that night.

After eating, Ulla felt she needed to get away from the others. Or maybe she wanted to get away from Cord. Either way she decided she was going to take a nap until the wagon train started again. "Will is nodding here in my lap and making me sleepy. If nobody minds, I think I'll take a nap with the children."

Becky crossed her arms over her chest. "I'm not sleepy, Mama. I don't want to take a nap."

"If you don't want to sleep, will you come in the wagon with Will and me and read a book?"

She thought a minute. "I guess I could do that since Joe don't want to play with me."

Joe eyed her. "Mama said she'd take me to play with Carney. We don't want no girls because we're going to play ball. Girls don't know how."

"See Mama, he don't want to play with me."

Ulla ignored the remark about Joe not wanting to play with her. "I still want you in the wagon with me. I don't know if I can nap if you're not there."

Cord spoke up. "Listen to your Mama, honey. I'd feel better if you were here with her, too. Besides, I know you enjoy your books."

"Oh, all right." Becky moved toward the wagon.

Ulla stood and carried Will with her. She didn't know Cord had followed until he moved beside her and lifted Becky inside. "I'll hand you Will, Becky, then I'll help your Mama inside."

"I can get in."

"I'm sure you can, but I'm going to help you."

Ulla sighed. "Whatever you say, Cord."

Whenever she was inside, he said, "Have a nice nap, Ulla."

"Wake me when it's time to pull out again."

He nodded and walked away.

Ulla cuddled down beside Will. It was all she could do to keep from crying, but she knew she couldn't do that. Not only would it upset Becky, but it would show she was still upset about Cord's feelings on the subject of love. And she didn't want him or anyone else to know that his take on the subject was breaking her heart.

~ * ~

Three days later, Cord walked up as Ulla finished the evening milking. He reached for the cow's tether. "It looks like it's coming up a storm so I'll take her to the grazing area and hobble her for the night."

She muttered a thank you and he watched as she walked over to the chairs where Ivy sat with Will on her lap. As she took a seat beside her friend, he heard her say, "Thanks for watching Will. Ivy. I'll take him now."

"Mama," Will muttered. "Cow."

Ivy laughed. "He's been saying those two words as he watched you attend to the cow. I'm not sure which is more exciting to him, seeing the cow or waiting for his mama to come and take him."

Ulla reached toward him and said, "Come on, big boy. Mama's ready to hold you."

Cord bit his lip as he stepped far enough away that he could no longer hear the conversation. He wondered how Ulla could have changed so quickly. Though she was polite and kind and never said anything harsh to him, he felt a strain between them. She was still her sweet self—open and gentle with Will and Becky, but noticeably distant with him. He figured he'd done or said something that had offended her, but for the life of him, he couldn't imagine what it was. Nothing had changed with him. He was still glad he married the woman and brought her along as a mother to Will and Becky. He was sure she understood this, so it couldn't be that she questioned his motives about the wedding.

He wondered if it could be that she questioned her own motives concerning the situation. Maybe she regretted marrying him or maybe she regretted leaving her home in Independence to come on this arduous trip. Or both. He shook his head. *I sure wish I could figure it out, then I could apologize to her and things could go back to what they were before. I want it that way because I honestly hadn't felt as contented in years as I have since I met her. I want that feeling around Ulla again.*

"Hello there, Dermott," a voice pulled him from his thoughts.

Cord nodded. "Doctor Guggenheim. When did you get back to the train?"

"Just a little while ago. I was trying to beat the gathering storm."

"How's the Kingston boy?"

"Got him settled in the hospital and under a doctor's care. I think when he and his family can cope with the fact he'll be a cripple for the rest of his life, he'll be all right."

"It was a tragic thing, but I'm sure they're happy he's alive." Cord staked the cow. "I'm also sure Naomi and your boys are glad to have you and your daughter back."

Saul chuckled. "Said they were."

"We're sure glad you've returned. Never know when you're going to need a good doctor."

"Not feeling poorly, are you?"

Cord chuckled. "Not me, but there are several children on this train and you know how they are. The sniffles can crop up at any time."

"That's a fact, but most of the mamas I know can handle them without my help." He started off. "I better get back to the family. See you later, Cord."

Cord watched him walk away. He couldn't help wondering if the man had some medical cure for the way Ulla had been acting. He then laughed at himself for such a crazy notion and hurried toward his wagon because he'd felt the first raindrop.

Ten

The wind began to pick up and Ulla tucked Will on one hip and carried her chair to hang on the side of the wagon. When she turned, she called, "Come here, Becky."

Becky looked out from the Nettleton's wagon. "Why, Mama?"

"It's going to rain and we need to get into our wagon."

"Can't I stay here and play with Joe and Springer?"

"Joe will be getting in his own wagon. Now come on."

She put her arms across her chest. "I don't want to."

"Listen to your mama, Becky," Cord's voice came from the edge of the clearing.

"Oh, Daddy. Tell Mama to let me stay here."

Ulla glanced at Cord, but didn't say anything.

He gave her a half smile, then turned toward his daughter. "No, Becky. Your Mama said to come to the wagon. Now, mind her."

Joe looked at her. "My mama's telling me to come inside our wagon, Becky. When I go, you'll be alone."

Becky stuck her mouth out and said, "I'd be with Springer."

"If it rains hard, Mama will let me take Springer in the wagon. You'll be by yourself then."

125

Becky didn't look happy, but she headed to her wagon without arguing any more.

The rain was coming down a little harder when Ulla watched Cord lift her into the back of the wagon. He then turned and reached for Will and sat him over the tailgate. "Watch him until I get Mama inside, Becky."

"I can climb in," Ulla muttered.

"I know, but I don't mind helping you." He put his hands on her waist and lifted her into the wagon.

She was angry with herself for being excited by his touch. To keep him from knowing, she moved next to the children. A crack of thunder followed by lightning made both of them jump into her arms.

"I'm scared," Becky whispered in her neck.

Will began to cry.

Cord climbed in the wagon and dropped beside them. "Don't be afraid, Becky. I'm here and I'll protect all of you."

She moved into her father's arms. "I'm glad you're here, Daddy, but I'm scared. Are you scared, Mama?"

Ulla wasn't sure what to say, so she nodded and mumbled, "A little." She then tried to calm Will with soft words. "It's going to be fine, Will. Nothing is going to hurt you."

She kissed the top of his head, but he continued to cry.

"I won't cry, Daddy," Becky said and snuggled in Cord's arm. "I know you won't let anything happen to us, but I'm a little afraid."

"Don't be, sweetheart. We're all safe here."

Thunder boomed again. Will clung to Ulla and wailed.

Cord's voice was harsh when he said, "Hush up, Will. You'll be fine."

Ulla glared at him because she couldn't understand how he could he be so comforting to Becky and fuss at his little son for being afraid. It wasn't right for him to use his severe voice to Will and be so sweet and calming with Becky. It made it obvious to her that he preferred one offspring over the other. She didn't understand it, but it was something she was going to confront him about as soon as they were alone. Now was not the time, so for the moment she hugged Will to her breast and began singing a soothing lullaby.

~ * ~

Cord knew he'd messed up again as he watched Ulla turn her accusing eyes from him to Will. He knew he shouldn't have yelled at the boy, but it was damn hard to control his temper when every time he looked at Will, he remembered that Yankee in Lisa's bed and the fact the enemy could very well be Will's father.

Would Ulla be more understanding and accepting if he explained the facts behind his feelings about the child to her? Would she agree that it was hard for him to show Will the same love and care he showed Becky? Or would she say he was an adult and he should accept Will as his own and forget about the lieutenant. If so, he knew he couldn't do that. He'd tried and it hadn't worked. In fact, he'd wished more than one time that he'd left Will in Atlanta. But if he had, there would have always been the question—is the boy of my seed? A question that could never be answered. Only Lisa knew the truth.

Ulla's song turned into a soft hum and he glanced at her. Her eyes were looking down upon the baby in her arms. And he had to admit that in many ways, Will was still a baby. One not responsible for his conception, but one who would never question his parentage as long as Cord called him his son. One who would only know Ulla as his mother and would have no feeling for the woman who had given him birth. Nor would he have any feeling for the Yankee soldier who may have been the man whose seed he evolved from. A man who the child would never know existed.

Then there was Becky, his beautiful daughter who was young enough to start forgetting much about her birth mother. Eventually the memories she did have would become sketchy and she would come to love and depend on Ulla as her only mother, too.

The four of them would be a family. That was, unless Ulla decided she didn't want to build a future with him. He knew she would have no trouble relating to and loving the children, but would she ever care enough about him to become a real wife? At first he thought she would, but now he wondered. He couldn't help recalling the way she'd reacted to him in the last few days. Oh, she had been pleasant enough, but she seemed to try not to be alone with him and she dodged talking about anything personal if they ended up close together. In fact, she'd avoided all conversations with him unless it had something to do with the children or the trip or what needed to be done during the day.

And here they sat in the back of the wagon with a storm raging around them and she wouldn't even look at him, much less, talk to him. Instead she sang to the children. Well, to Will anyway. It just so happened her soft voice carried over to Becky's ears. Not only that, Will had not only quit crying, but he'd gone to sleep. And Becky had curled up on the mattress beside him as she fell into sleep, too.

Damn if her voice isn't so sweet, I'm getting drowsy myself.

He watched as Ulla gently placed Will down beside her, then glanced up. When their eyes met, she whispered, "Why, Cord?"

He frowned. "Why what, Ulla?"

"Why do you make such a difference between your children?"

Damn, she got to the point, didn't she? What should he say? Should he tell her why it was impossible for him to relate to Will as he did Becky? Would she understand? He had a feeling she probably would not.

He decided the best thing he could do was lie. "I don't know what you mean, Ulla."

"Then, Cord, you're not the man I thought you were when I agreed to marry you." She turned from him and cuddled down beside Will.

Though she kept her voice low, he couldn't help hearing her whisper in Will's ear, "Don't worry, my precious. Someday your father will realize what a wonderful little boy you are. I just hope it's not too late when he does."

~ * ~

The next day was strained between them, though neither said anything short or hateful to the other. It was as if they were afraid to say anything.

While the men were taking care of the livestock at the nooning, Ivy walked up to Ulla. "Are you all right, my friend?"

Ulla forced a smile. "Of course. Why do you ask?"

"I can't help noticing how you and Cord are side-stepping each other. Have you had your first fight?"

Ulla shook her head. "No. Nothing is wrong."

Ivy persisted. "Don't be ashamed if you've had words. It happens to all couples. When Pete came home, he and I often had little arguments."

"I never hear you arguing."

"We seldom do now, but it was difficult then. Pete was moody and resentful of the way he was treated by the people in Independence. He felt he'd paid for his mistake and he thought people should realize that. I had expected him to come home and be the same man he was when he was sent away and in ways he was, but in others he wasn't. Prison had made him unsure of who he could trust and who he couldn't. He even felt that about me at times. If it hadn't been for Joe, I'm not sure we would've made it."

"But you seem so happy, Ivy."

"We are now, but it took a few months for us to find our meeting ground. We've been married a little over a year and I can tell you without reserve that we're a very happy couple. I can't imagine life without him and I'm positive he feels the same about me."

"I can only wish that will happen for us."

"It will, Ulla. All you have to do is sit together and talk it out. First tell him exactly what you're thinking and feeling, then ask him to tell you what he thinks. I know it's hard for a man to tell you about his feelings, but if you persist, he'll do it."

Ulla was thoughtful for a minute, then she turned to Ivy. "Maybe I shouldn't have married Cord so quickly."

"Don't think like that. Cord is a good man and you and he are wonderful together. You just have to get over these little bumps in the marriage."

Again Ulla was quiet a minute. Finally she asked, "I can't understand why Cord makes such a difference in the way he treats his children. He's always sweet and kind to Becky, but he acts as if he doesn't even love Will. Even Becky told me she thought her father loved her better than he did her brother."

Ivy frowned. "I have to admit, I've noticed him be a little harsher with Will. He may not even be aware of it himself, but sometimes men will be nicer to a girl child because they feel the boy is a threat for some reason."

"Oh, Ivy, how could anyone think of sweet little Will as a threat?"

"That's a question you need to discuss with Cord."

"I suppose you're right. But the way he treats Will is only one thing I didn't know about Cord before I married him."

"He isn't mean to you, is he?"

"Oh, no. He's been nothing but kind to me."

"Then...here the men come. Just think about what I said. Try talking to him."

Ulla nodded. "If I can work up the courage, I'll try."

"Hello, ladies," Pete said. "Hope the coffee is hot."

"It is." Ivy moved to the campfire. "Want a cup, Cord?"

"I sure do. We've had a rough time with a couple of ornery oxen. For a while there I thought we were going to have to put them down, but they finally settled."

Ulla felt a sudden fear. "Nobody was hurt, were they?"

Cord shook his head. "Everyone is like Pete and me, just tired from tussling with the beast."

"What happened?" Ivy asked as she handed the men cups of coffee.

"Thank you, honey, and to answer your question...an ox turned on its owner and then on the other animals. It wasn't long until all the oxen seemed to be in on it. It took a while to calm them down."

"Thank you, Ivy." Cord turned to Ulla. "Where is..." he hesitated, then said, "where are the children?"

Ulla knew he'd purposely corrected himself. She was sure that at first he was going to ask where Becky was. He must have thought she'd be even more distant to him if he didn't include both children. She decided to ignore it this time. "Becky and Joe have gone to play with the Maloney children and Will's asleep."

"It's time for the children to come back. Come with me, Pete. Let's go get them."

Pete gave Ivy a puzzled look and started to say something.

She didn't give him a chance. "It's been a while since we took a walk together. I want you to come along and hold my hand."

Pete drained his coffee cup, set it aside and took his wife's hand. "I can't turn down an offer like that. We'll be back soon."

Ulla glanced at Cord and muttered, "They couldn't have been more obvious, could they?"

"I'm sure they still think of us as newlyweds that would like to have their time alone together."

After a minute, Ulla said, "Ivy noticed that we have been a little standoffish with each other. She asked me if we'd had our first fight."

"Have we, Ulla?"

"No, Cord. The last thing I want to do is fight with you. I just want to know what you're thinking at times and why you do things that are so contradictory to the good man I know you are."

"You're talking about the way I relate to the children, aren't you?"

"That's one thing."

He raised an eyebrow. "What else could you have on your mind?"

"We'll discuss that later. I think the most pressing things on my mind are Will and the way you treat him. From what I can see, in his little boy way, he loves you dearly and for the life of me I don't understand how can you not be as attentive to that sweet little boy as you are to Becky?"

She glanced at Cord and noticed how his jaw had begun to work as if he were gritting his teeth. After waiting a few minutes of silence, she thought he wasn't going to give her an answer and wondered if she should press him for one.

He finally broke the silence. "I don't know if you'll understand even if I try to explain it to you."

Ulla reached over and touched his arm. "Please try, Cord."

He nodded. "Let me get another cup of coffee and I'll try. Would you like one?"

"Yes. Thank you."

When he returned, he handed her a cup of coffee and pulled his chair closer to her. "I'm not sure where to begin."

"It doesn't matter where you start, Cord. Just beginning is the important thing."

"Then I'm going to tell you straight out. I have good reason to believe Will was sired by another man. I know for a fact that Becky is my daughter, but I don't know whether or not Will is my son."

Ulla was stunned. Of all the things Cord could have told her, this was something that had never entered her mind. For a few seconds she was lost for words. She then muttered, "I'm sorry, Cord, but you do know Will can't help that."

"I know he can't, Ulla. I also know I'm the only father he'll ever know. That's why I feel guilty every time I snap at him, but I can't seem to help myself. Every time I look at him, I think of that damn Yankee."

Ulla was confused, but she didn't have a chance to question him any further. A scream followed by two rapid gunshots from the wagon in front of them stopped her.

Cord jumped up and ran to the wagon. He grabbed his gun off the peg on the side. "Get inside and I'll see what's going on."

She didn't argue and let him lift her inside. She wanted to get to Will as soon as she could. She knew Becky was safe with Pete and Ivy.

~ * ~

"What the hell's going on, Reed?" Cord demanded when he came around the wagon and saw his neighbor standing there with a gun in his hand. Pete ran up behind him.

Sam pointed the rifle toward the area at the edge of the camp ground. "Damn rattlesnake. Scared Beulah so bad I thought she was gonna keel right over on me."

"Did anyone get bitten?"

"No. Beulah saw it and was far enough away it couldn't strike her. Trina and Leo had walked up a few wagons to visit with a couple of friends of theirs. Just me and Beulah here."

Cord holstered his pistol and so did Pete. Pete said, "Glad you got him. I know how afraid of snakes Ivy is and I'd hate for her to see one this close to where we're sleeping."

Cord nodded. "Probably the same for Ulla. I bet from now on she'll insist on all of us sleeping in the wagon instead of the tents."

"Cord," Ulla called. "Is everyone all right?"

A panting Beulah walked up. "I'll go talk to her, Cord. You men get that thing out of my sight before I get back or Leo and Trina decide to come back, too."

In a matter of minutes a crowd had gathered, but soon dispersed when they found out the excitement was only a dead rattlesnake.

When Cord returned to the wagon, he found Ulla sitting there rocking Will.

"The gunshots woke him and he began crying for me. Ivy tried to quiet him, but he only wanted his mama."

"You're very good with him, Ulla. Just like a real mama would be."

She gave him a hard look. "I am his real mama from now on, Cord. I love him just as much as if I'd given him birth."

He wondered if she wanted to ask, '*Why can't you do the same?*' He only said, "He's a lucky guy to be loved so much by you. I better get things ready to start moving again." He turned and climbed back out of the wagon without saying anything else or waiting for her to answer.

Eleven

Nothing much changed in Cord and Ulla's relationship. They still tried to be polite to each other and she could tell he was trying harder not to be harsh with Will. But to her he wasn't trying hard enough. She thought he should just forget about the Yankee, whoever he was and whatever he had to do with Will's birth. Cord hadn't mentioned the previous conversation and she was trying to work up the courage to bring it up again.

Two days later, the train camped by a good sized creek. Ulla wasn't sure what the name of it was or even if it had one. She was simply thrilled that at last there was a place to wash their soiled clothes and then take some of the dirt and grime off her body. Naomi told her that Mr. Pruitt said there was a nice pool above the waterfall where the women would have privacy to take a bath and relax.

She and Ivy made plans to go as soon as they put the dried beans that had been soaking all day in the pot to cook, had the children bathed and had their laundry hanging on the makeshift clothesline the men had constructed for them. After gathering clean underclothes and a red and black checked dress, Ulla turned to Cord. "If it's not too much trouble, will you please watch Will while I'm bathing?"

"Yes, Ulla. I'll watch him."

"Becky will be here to help you. She took a bath while I was doing the wash."

He nodded. "Go and enjoy your bath."

"Thank you. I won't be long."

He nodded.

Ulla sighed and joined Ivy. "I suppose the children will be safe with them."

Ivy laughed. "Don't worry, Ulla. They'll be fine and we need a break. It doesn't hurt the men to watch them now and again."

"I suppose you're right."

It wasn't long until they reached the area Mr. Pruitt had told Naomi about. "Oh my," Ulla's eyes grew big. It's lovely here."

"Yes it is and I'm looking forward to getting this tired old body in water to my neck."

Ulla laughed. "So am I. It seems like forever since I had a real bath."

"Me, too."

"Do you regret coming on this trek, Ivy?"

Ivy shook her head. "Not at all. In fact, I don't think I've ever seen Pete as relaxed and happy as he has been since we left Independence. Even with all the hardships, coming with you was the best decision we ever made."

"I'm happy for you and I hope it hasn't been too hard."

"It hasn't, but there is one thing I haven't told anyone. Not even Pete."

Ulla frowned. "What's that?"

"You'll probably notice when I take my clothes off that I'm getting a little thick around the middle."

Ulla continued to frown. "I don't see how you can gain weight no more than we eat and the way we're having to work along with the men."

"It's not from overeating, Ulla."

"Then what?" It then dawned on Ulla. "You're pregnant."

Ivy nodded. "I knew before we left Independence, but I also knew Pete wouldn't let me make the trip if he knew."

"Oh, Ivy. I hope you don't have any trouble because of traveling like this."

"So far, I'm fine. I just know I'm not going to be able to hide it from him much longer. I just want to wait until we're far enough away that he doesn't insist on going back. You won't tell him, will you?"

"You sound like you're happy about the baby and for that reason, I won't tell him a thing."

"I am happy. I was afraid I'd never be able to give Pete another child and he missed so much when Joe was born."

Ulla smiled at her friend. "Then, if you're happy, I'm happy for you."

They stopped at the bank and disrobed. As they stepped into the water, Ivy asked, "How about you, Ulla? Are you glad you came on this trip?"

Ulla gave her a slight smile. "I didn't have any other choice, Ivy."

"Are you sure?"

"I'm positive." She splashed water toward her friend.

Ivy laughed. "I'll get you for that." She splashed water right back.

"Would you look at that?" Charlene's voice came from the bank.

"Two grown women acting just like kids." Naomi answered.

Ulla looked around and saw Naomi and Charlene standing there laughing at them. "You two stop making fun of us and come on in. The water is great."

It wasn't long until almost every woman from the train was in the water. For the first time in several days, Ulla felt happy and relaxed. She knew there would still be the strain between Cord and her when she went back to the wagon, but for the time being she could relax and forget the tension between her and the man who called himself her husband.

~ * ~

"Pete, we haven't had a chance for a serious talk lately without the wives around."

"That's true. What do you have on your mind, Cord?"

"How's your family doing?"

"We're fine. Why do you ask?"

"To be honest, Becky said the other night that she heard you and Ivy yelling at each other."

Pete chuckled. "As a matter of fact, we had a few words, but it was nothing serious."

"Are you sure? I'd hate to think that since you came on this trip to help Ulla it's her fault you were fighting."

"Not at all. I'll be honest. I was talking to Pruitt the other day and he said there was a fairly new town in Wyoming Territory called Winton Crossing that has been growing for about five years. He said it was a pretty nice place. I mentioned to Ivy that if they didn't have a handy man, they might be interested in having one. If there is one already, they might be some other job I could do to support my family. She put me straight in a few choice words. Said we agreed to go to Oregon and we owed it to Ulla to go all the way. I realize she was right. I guess I was anxious to set up a business and get on with being a family where nobody would hold my past against Ivy and Joe."

"I'm glad it wasn't anything more serious."

"Not at all. Ivy and I may have a few words now and then, but out love is strong enough to get over them."

Cord lifted an eyebrow. He didn't want to get into a discussion about love. "Tell me about this town."

"I don't know a lot more than I told you."

"Maybe I'll check with Pruitt."

Pete gave him a curious look. "Why would you be interested?"

"I may not be, but it could be worth looking into. I'm the one who said we were going to Oregon because that's the destination of this train, but if Ulla doesn't care, who's to say we have to go to there? If we came to a nice town to live in, I might decide it's a better place to settle down with my family."

"What would Ulla think of that?"

"Of course I'd ask her, but I don't think she'd be opposed to it. She just wanted to get away from her uncle and aunt in Independence."

"Then why don't we find out a little more about this place before we make any kind of decision about it?"

"I agree. We should do that."

Pete looked around. "I wonder how much longer they're going to be gone."

Cord pulled out his pocket watch. "They must be enjoying their baths. It's been a little over an hour since they left."

"They'll probably come back as wrinkled as an old prune."

"You'd better watch talk like that, my dear husband." Ivy walked up and tapped his shoulder. "Ulla and I are all fresh and pretty and had a wonderful time. What did you two do?"

"Just sat around and talked." He grinned at Ivy.

Cord looked at Ulla. "I must say, you look fresh and pretty."

"Thank you." She gave him a shy smile. "Where are the children?"

"Playing under the Nettletons' wagon."

She looked in that direction. "I see Becky and Joe, but I don't see Will."

"He's around there somewhere. Becky said she'd watch him." Cord called, "Becky, where's your brother?"

"He kept messing with the things Joe and I had set up to play with so I told him to leave us alone and go stay with you."

Cord and Pete jumped up at the same time as Ulla ran toward the Nettleton wagon.

~ * ~

Ulla's heart pounded as she bent to look under the wagon. "Will, baby, where are you?"

Cord was on her heels. "Do you see him?"

She whirled around and glared at him. "How could you not notice he wasn't here?"

Cord reached for her arm. "Ulla, I didn't ..."

She jerked her arm away. "Don't try to defend your actions to me. Just find him."

"Maybe we should check the river," Pete suggested.

Cord nodded and looked at Ulla. "You stay here, we'll find him."

"No!" She snapped at him then turned to Ivy as Cord and Pete walked away. "Please watch Becky. I have to find my little boy."

Becky skipped up. "Can I go find Will? Joe will help."

Ulla took the child's shoulder and said in a firm voice, "Listen to me, Becky. You're not going anywhere. You stay here and do exactly what Miss Ivy says."

"But…"

"Don't argue with me. If you do, I'll have to punish you. Now go with Miss Ivy."

Becky's eyes got big. "Are you mad at me?"

Ulla ignored her and walked away. At the moment she didn't want to take the time to explain the gravity of what had happened to the precocious little girl. She had to find Will.

She made a quick tour around the wagons; then with her heart feeling as if it would rip from her chest, she headed toward the river. She prayed the hardest she'd ever prayed in her life and knew if anything happened to the little boy she'd never forgive herself for leaving him with his irresponsible sister and a father who didn't seem to care whether he was around or not.

By the time she got to the river, several men and a couple of women had joined the search. Not only were they going up and down the banks of the water, but some were moving into the weeds to look. One woman suggested they check all the wagons to make sure he hadn't taken up with some child and was innocently playing without a thought of how worried his mother was. Another man said he was going to check around the corral because someone told him Will liked to pet the cows.

Ulla's heart sank when she heard this. Her baby could be trampled to death without realizing how dangerous the horses, cows and oxen were. She almost followed the man, but decided she wanted to check the river herself.

When she reached the bank, she looked into the water. At first it had seemed soothing and relaxing. She had even enjoyed squatting beside the running water and washing their clothes. Now the stream seemed huge and threating. It held all kinds of dangers—rocks, jagged wedges of tree limbs and probably water snakes. Any of them would not only entice a little boy, but they could kill him, too.

She had worked herself into in a near panic when she glanced up and realized she was following Pete and Cord. At first, for some strange reason, she wanted to cry out for her husband to comfort her. On the other hand, she wanted to scream at him for not taking better care of their precious little boy. Didn't he realize Will was still almost a baby? Did he think at six years old, Becky was old enough to take on the responsibility of watching after an active toddler who had only recently learned to walk away from everyone?

She opened her mouth to scream at him when his voice floated to her. "I'm going up to the pool above the waterfall, Pete."

"Do you really think he could have gotten that far?"

"I don't know, but there's the possibility he decided to go find his mother."

"Did he know which way she went?"

"Yeah. He was crying for her as she walked away with Ivy. I didn't want her to hear how pitiful he sounded because I knew she'd come back and not go enjoy her bath with the other women. That's why I told him he could go play with Becky."

"Why don't I check around the falls?"

"Oh God, don't let him be there. I'll never forgive myself if..."

Ulla was stunned when she heard Cord's voice begin to choke. Maybe he did care more for Will than he showed. Or maybe he only felt guilty for not watching the boy more closely.

It was then she looked at the falls. They weren't huge. There were two streams about a foot wide as the trickled over the rocks, but they landed on a large grouping of jagged rocks. Rocks where a child's boot was caught in an eddy and continued to whirl around going nowhere.

"No!" Ulla screamed and fainted.

~ * ~

"Take care of your wife. I'll go." Pete ran down the bank.

Cord nodded and rushed to Ulla. Squatting on the ground, he lifted her into his arms and held her close to his chest. Tears filled his eyes as he thought about the little boy whose shoe floated in the water. The little boy that loved him and called him Daddy. The little boy who had no idea his father's selfishness wouldn't let himself love his child. And now that it was too late...he knew in spite of Will's conception, he loved the little boy with all his heart, a heart that felt as if it were going to split open at this moment.

"Oh, Ulla, what have I done? How could I have...?" He frowned.

The sound of a child's cry interrupted his words.

He looked around as Ulla began to come to. "Cord. Oh, Cord, it can't be so."

Cord's heart pounded against her and he swallowed. "Ulla, calm down."

"How can I calm down? My little boy..."

"No, Ulla. Look over there." He pointed to the side of the waterfall.

Ulla gasped. "It's Will. He's on that limb. I've got to get him." She struggled to pull herself out of Cord's arms.

"No, Ulla. I'll get him."

Pete returned. "It was only a boot."

"I know." Though Cord wanted to rush to the bent tree to rescue Will, he made himself think logically. Standing, he motioned for Liam Mahoney.

"Yeah, Cord."

"I've got to get my boy. Find a rope and try to keep everyone quiet. I don't want to scare Will. He could fall into the water and land on those rocks if he gets excited."

"Oh, Cord. Please save him."

"I will, Ulla." He leaned over and kissed her and started toward the base of the leaning tree.

Ulla clung to his arm and walked with him. "Be careful."

"I will, honey." He paused and hugged her against him. "You stay right here where you can watch and say prayers for us."

"I will. Please be careful. I want you both to be safe."

It seemed the next minutes lasted for an hour. Several people came running to watch the attempted rescue and surprisingly, they were all quiet. Naomi Guggenheim arrived and moved beside Ulla. "Don't worry about her, Cord. I'll see she's all right. You're going to have enough on your mind."

"Thank you, Naomi." He gave Ulla another quick kiss and turned so Pete could secure the rope around his chest and under his arms. He then climbed the tree to the area where it leaned over the falls. All the time he was petitioning God to please keep the little boy safe until he could reach him.

As he stepped onto the branch that held his son, he said in a soothing voice, "Will, Daddy wants you to sit very still until he gets to you."

Will looked at his father, grinned and raised his arms. "Daddy?"

"Yes, sweetheart. Please don't move."

Cord was sure he heard the limb crack. "Let me reach him before this limb goes, God. Please. He's just a little boy and deserves to live. Let me save Will for Ulla."

"Where Mama?"

Keeping his voice as calm as he couldm Cord said, "I'll take you to Mama, Will. Just sit still until I reach you."

Will leaned over and Cord's heart sank as he saw his child begin to slip. The space on the limb between him and the child seemed to grow longer instead of letting him get closer. There were a couple of cracks and Cord knew it wasn't going to hold much longer.

Then he was beside his son. He grabbed the child. "Put your arms around Daddy's neck, Will."

The little boy giggled and hugged Cord tightly and muttered, "Love Daddy."

With a thankful heart, Cord began to back up, but there was a sharp snap. He knew the limb was going and the last thing he remembered was hearing Ulla scream and feeling Will pat his face and giggle.

~ * ~

Ulla wanted to cover her eyes, but she couldn't as she watched the limb fall from under Cord. She screamed, but couldn't tear her eyes away as she watched her husband dangle on the rope with Will clutched in his arms. It was as if in slow motion, the rope slammed Cord against the rock wall behind the falls. Somehow the man managed to turn so his side hit the rocks, keeping Will safe.

People ran as the man and his son went under the water at the bottom of the falls. By the time Ulla reached them, someone handed her a crying Will and someone else had pulled an unconscious Cord to the side of the bank.

Ulla hugged Will to her and tried to get to Cord, but somebody held her back. "Wait, honey. Dr. Guggenheim is here. He needs to look after Cord now."

She recognized her friend Charlene's voice and shook her head. "He's hurt and I need to be with him."

"You will be, Ulla. Let's head toward the wagon."

"No."

Naomi joined them. When she spoke her voice was calm and soothing. "Let me have Will, Ulla. I'm sure Saul will insist that the men carry Cord to your wagon. Don't you want to be there when they bring him?"

A shiver ran down Ulla's spine. "Are you trying to get me away from here because Cord is dead?"

"Cord's not dead, Ulla, but he is hurt. Now come along. Let's get the wagon ready so we can put him to bed."

"No. You go get it ready. I need to be with my husband."

"Mama!" Will reached for her and cried.

Ulla kissed Will's forehead. "Go with Miss Naomi, sweetheart. Mama will be there soon."

"Ulla..."

"No, Naomi. I'm not leaving until I know how Cord is." She glanced around at Charlene. "Please go help her. There are mattresses in the back of our wagon. Please get a bed ready for Cord."

As her friends left with Will, Ulla tapped a man on the shoulder. "Please let me by."

He nodded and she saw she was on the opposite side of Cord from where Saul was working on him. She dropped to her knees beside her husband and sobbed. Blood soaked the cloth the doctor had tied to the left side of Cord's face and head. A bone in his left arm stuck through the tear where his shirt had been torn away.

Though she didn't want to let the idea into her mind, she couldn't help asking, "Is Cord dying?"

"He's alive, Ulla, but he's in pretty bad shape." Saul looked at her. "We need to get him to the wagon."

"Of course."

"Pete grab his shoulders and Rayburn, you get his feet. Try to keep him as level as you can. Watch his arm. I'll set that, but I don't want to disturb anything else that might be broken." He turned back to Ulla. "I know you're upset, but try to be calm. That's the best way you can help him right now."

"I'll try."

Beulah came up and put an arm around Ulla's shoulders, but didn't try to pull her away from her husband. They walked beside the men carrying Cord, and Ulla let her eyes linger on Cord's face. His usual dark complexion was paler than she ever thought a living human's would be. *Oh, my dear merciful God, please let him recover. I didn't realize how much I loved him until I saw him risk his life to save our son. Please reward him with more years to spend with his family. I know he loves his son. He may have not realized it, but he's always cared. He wouldn't have risked his life to save Will's if he hadn't cared. Oh, God, all I can do is leave him in your hands, but you know how I love him and want to be his wife and not in name only. I want to give him more children and for us to live to see grandchildren. But, God, if it's not to be, don't let him suffer. Please wrap him in your love and your mercy.*

Cord moaned.

"Oh, no, Saul. He's hurting."

"Yes, he is, but he won't remember the pain if he makes it."

Ulla gave him a sharp look. "What do you mean, if he makes it?"

"I'm going to do my best to pull him through, Ulla, but a lot will depend on whether or not he has internal injuries."

Before she could say anything else, they reached the wagon and she stood back as they placed Cord inside. Saul climbed in behind him. Ulla started to follow, but Naomi put her hand on Ulla's shoulder. "Here, honey, take Will. Saul might need my help."

"But…"

A crying Becky came running up and threw her arms around Ulla. "Is my Daddy dead?"

Ulla took a deep breath, shifted Will to her left hip and put her free arm around the child. "No, darling. Doctor Saul is helping him."

"But I heard a man say Daddy was dying." Becky tried to get to the tailgate of the wagon.

Ulla held her back. "I want to climb in the wagon, too, Becky, but the doctor needs to work on your daddy. We would be in the way."

"I won't …"

"You wouldn't want to be in there and be in the way of the doctor helping Daddy, would you?"

She shook her head.

"Tell you what, you get us a chair and we'll sit here close to the wagon so when the doctor gets through, we can climb inside and see Daddy."

"Okay." In a minute she was back with two chairs. There were still tears in her eyes. "I don't want Daddy to die, Mama."

"I don't either, Becky."

Ivy approached them.

"Ulla, would you like for me to take Will and Becky?"

"I want to stay with Mama," Becky said.

"Mama." Will giggled and patted Ulla's face. "Daddy fall."

"Yes, darling. Daddy fall." She looked up at her friend. "Thank you, Ivy, but I think I'll keep the children with me."

"I understand. Kathleen just came up and said she'd take care of Becky when you want her to. Charlene and Beulah and I will be close by if you need us."

"I appreciate that."

It wasn't long until Will went to sleep in Ulla's arms. She nodded to Ivy to come get him. After he was secure and asleep in the Nettletons' wagon, Becky whispered, "Do you think I'm too old to sit in your lap?"

"Absolutely not." Ulla held out her arms. "Come here."

Becky climbed in her lap and looked up. "When I wanted to sit in her lap, my grandma Anderson said I was too big for laps and I had to always sit in a chair and act like a lady."

"Well, as your mama, I say you can sit in my lap whenever you want to."

"Does that mean you still love me, Mama?"

Ulla hugged her close. "Of course, I love you, Becky. What made you think I didn't?"

"You were mad at me cause Will run away."

Ulla knew she had to concentrate on what she said. There was the possibility she was the only parent the child might have after today.

No, she scolded herself. Cord is going to be fine and we'll all be happy again. "Becky, I wasn't mad. I was scared. I would have been the same way if you had disappeared. A mama gets frightened when something happens to one of her children. She might say something she wouldn't otherwise say."

Becky hugged Ulla's neck. "I'm glad you still love me, Mama. I love you and I'm sorry I let Will get gone."

"Your daddy found Will before I did and your little brother is fine. Now, you relax and we won't talk about it anymore."

"Where did Daddy find Will?"

"He was down at the river. I think he was trying to find me."

"I'm glad Daddy found him."

"Me, too."

There was a pause. Then Becky said, "I hope Daddy gets well."

"Me, too, sweetheart. Me, too."

They were interrupted when Naomi climbed out of the wagon. "I think you should come inside, Ulla."

Ulla's heart lurched as she stood and sat Becky on her feet. "Is he..."

Kathleen walked up. "Becky, you come with me and..."

"I want to go with Mama."

"You can go later, honey," Naomi said. "Mama needs to see your daddy alone. You go with Kathleen and check on Will."

"He's asleep."

"We'll make sure." Naomi took one of Becky's hands and Kathleen took the other. They walked away.

Ulla rushed to the back of the wagon with a prayer on her lips. *Oh, God. Please don't let Cord be dead or dying. The children and I need him. Please God. Please.*

Twelve

Cord lay on the mattress with the lower half of his body covered to his waist with a sheet. A bandage on his head has spots of blood on it and his left arm was wrapped and in a sling. There were bruises on the left side of his face and upper body, especially his shoulder.

Ulla gasped. "Is he…"

"Don't panic, Ulla." Saul warned her. "He's in bad shape, but for the time being, he's alive."

"For the time being?"

"I've taken care of all his outward injuries, but I can't tell what's going on inside. He hit those rocks full force and he could have messed up any of his organs. It'll be a few days before we're sure he's all right inside." Saul shook his head. "He's a brave man. I'm sure he knew he was falling and deliberately turned so he'd hit the rocks instead of letting his boy take the impact. It's a good thing, too. If the child had hit this hard, it probably would've killed him."

"Oh, Saul." A tear ran down her cheek.

"Now, young lady, I didn't tell you this to upset you. Just wanted you to know what I thought happened. Now, get hold of yourself. It's going to take a lot of courage to help your husband through this."

"I'm sorry for being so weak. What can I do to help him?"

"Don't be sorry for your feelings. He's your man and I know how much you two care about each other. You're just going to have be the strong one until he's on his feet again."

"I understand and I will be strong."

He nodded. "Good. As you can see, his left side is where he's hurt the worst. I've set his broken arm and bandaged as many of the cuts and bruises as I could. His hip must have hit almost as hard as his left arm and shoulder and a lot of the skin is gone, but thank heavens, it's not broken. The bandage on it is going to need changing every day. You're going to have to do it if I'm not available."

"I can do that, Saul, but how about the other bandages?"

"The one on his head will need to be changed again soon because of the blood, but I'll do that tonight. It should then be fine until tomorrow." He sighed. "Naomi is getting some of the women to rip up a sheet so we'll have enough bandages."

"I have more sheets that can be used."

"You also have a couple of children and you'll need them for your beds. Most of us can spare at least one without any hardship."

"We won't need too many. I can wash the bandages."

"That's fine, Ulla. Wash them when you can, but you're not going to have many chances to do laundry." When she started to protest, he held up his hand. "The bandages are a small sacrifice for the people and it makes the women feel good to do something to help in situation like this. I'm going to see if I can round up enough men to get your wagon on its way."

"I hadn't thought of that, but I'm sure Pete will help."

"We'll all help as much as we can, so you won't have to do anything except take care of your husband." He patted her shoulder. "I'm going to my wagon now, but I'll come back before you bed down tonight. If you need me sooner, just send the word."

"I will, Saul. Thank you." She watched him climb out of the wagon, then she knelt beside Cord. Taking his right hand in hers, she whispered. "We'll get through this, my love. All you have to do is get well. I'll take care of everything else. Just don't leave me alone because the children and I need you."

It was then the silent tears began to fall in earnest.

~ * ~

Ulla didn't argue when Esther Guggenheim appeared and asked to take Becky to her wagon to spend the night. Will fell asleep in the Nettletons' wagon and Ivy insisted he be left there. After thinking it over, Ulla agreed it would be best. Cord had yet to regain full consciousness and she knew she'd be needed when he did.

When she settled on the mattress near him, she didn't think she'd be able to sleep, but she did doze. She was half in and half out of sleep when Cord's groans made her jerk awake. She rose up, lit the lantern and leaned over him. "Are you waking up, Cord?"

He opened an eye. "I hurt."

"I know. Let me get you something." She set the lantern on a trunk and reached for the medicine Saul had left.

Before she could open the bottle, Cord whispered, "I'm sorry, Ulla."

She frowned. "You have nothing to be sorry for, Cord."

"I tried to save him. I really wanted to." A tear appeared in his eye.

She wasn't sure if it was because of the pain or if he was talking about something else. "You did a brave..."

"I didn't realize until I thought he was going to die that I do love him." His voice grew raspy and weaker.

She continued to frown. "What are you talking about?"

He gasped for breath. "Why aren't you upset with me? I killed him."

"I don't know what you think you've done, Cord, but you didn't kill anyone."

"The limb broke...I...dropped ..." His voice trailed off.

"Do you think you dropped Will?"

There was no answer. Cord was again lost to reality.

Ulla touched his face and whispered, "Oh, Cord. You think Will is dead and it's your fault. But that's not so. Thanks to you, he's fine. I will explain everything to you when you wake up again."

She set the medicine back and blew out the lantern. At least maybe he could sleep naturally for a while. Though she knew it helped his pain, she didn't like him being in a drugged sleep. She wanted his mind clear so she could let him know what really happened on that tree branch over the falls. And what a hero he was to her and everyone else who saw the rescue.

The rest of the night passed with him sleeping. When the trumpet sounded for the morning readying to move the wagon train, Ulla jumped up and dressed quickly. Checking Cord to be sure he was still sleeping, she climbed out of the back of the wagon.

Ivy met her. "How is he, Ulla?"

"He's still out. He did wake up for a few minutes last night. He kept mumbling about how he'd killed Will."

"I'm sure you explained that Will was alive and well."

"I wanted to, but he went right back to sleep."

Ivy nodded. "I told Pete I'd be taking care of Will today so I couldn't help as much with the team."

"No, Ivy. I'll take care of Will. And Becky, too. The children will stay in the wagon with me."

"But what if Cord gets worse or, God forbid, he…" Ivy didn't finish her sentence.

"Cord is not going to die, Ivy. I don't believe God will take him away from us now. We need him."

"I hope you're right." Ivy put her hand on Ulla's arm. "Come and get some coffee and something to eat. Pete said he would hitch up your team and I think he said Eli Guggenheim is going to drive your wagon today. We'll be close if you need us."

Ulla nodded. "I need to milk the cow."

"Not this morning. Naomi said she was coming to milk it." Ivy poured a cup of coffee for her friend. "In fact, here she comes now. She has Becky with her."

Becky broke loose of Naomi's hand and ran. "Mama!"

Ulla held out her arms. "Come on, sweetheart."

Becky began to cry. "I wanted to come sleep with you, but they wouldn't let me."

"It's fine. You're here now. We need to eat a little then get Will. The three of us are going to ride in the wagon with your daddy today."

Becky stared at her. "I thought Daddy was dead."

"No, honey. He's not dead, but he's very sick. You're going to have to help me keep Will quiet so your daddy can rest."

"I will, Mama."

Ulla got Will from Ivy's wagon and she and the children ate breakfast together. She then watched as Saul arrived to check on Cord and change the bandages.

When he climbed out of the wagon, he put his hand on her shoulder. "He's holding his own, Ulla. It won't be easy, but try to keep him as comfortable as you can when we get started."

"I will, Saul."

"In case he wakes up and the pain is too much, I left some extra laudanum because you'll probably need it when the wagon starts to bump along the trail."

"Thanks, Saul. He woke up last night, but he didn't stay awake long. I didn't even have time to give him any medicine."

"That's a good sign, but he still has a long way to go, and I hope he wakes up more and more. Every day will help him get stronger, but I'm still not promising anything. It'll take a while to see if there are any injuries inside that we're unable to see."

"I understand, but I'm going to think positive. The children and I need him."

He smiled. "And he sure needs the three of you."

Pete came up with the mules. He hitched them to the Dermott wagon. Nodding to Ulla, he said, "I don't know if anyone told you, Ulla, but Saul's son, Eli will be coming to drive you."

Saul smiled at her. "He insisted he wanted to help out and I told him I could handle our team. He should be here soon."

"I hate to be so much trouble."

"It's no trouble, Ulla. We're all glad to help. I'll see you later today."

"Don't feel bad about needing help, Ulla. You know Ivy and I will be right behind you on the trail today. In case you need us or want anything, all you have to do is let us know."

"I know that and I appreciate it." She stood and held Will out to Ivy. "I think I'll get in the wagon now. Are you ready, Becky?"

"Yes, Mama."

"I'll give Will to you as soon as you're settled inside." Ivy followed her to the wagon.

In a few minutes, Ulla was settled on the mattress beside Cord and Becky sat beside her. Will cuddled in her lap, but he was quiet. Finally Becky broke the silence. "Mama, Daddy looks bad."

"He's very sick, honey, but we're going to take good care of him and he'll be better soon."

"Daddy fall," Will said.

Ulla pulled him close. "Yes, sweetheart. Daddy fall just so you would be safe. I'm so proud of him."

"I guess that means he really does love Will, don't it, Mama?"

"Yes, Becky. I'm sure that's exactly what it means." She smiled at her daughter. "Now why don't you get one of your books and read something. I'm sure Will would love to hear a story."

"Story."

"Yes, sweetheart. A story for you." She placed Will on the mattress beside Becky. "We should be leaving soon and I want to be able to help your father if he needs me."

"Yes, Mama." She turned to her little brother. "Now, Will, we have to be good and help Mama so she can help Daddy."

"Daddy."

"Yes. Now sit still and I'll read to you."

Ulla smiled and turned her attention to her husband. *Oh, Cord, I can't wait until you're yourself again so you can see how lucky we are to be parents. We have two wonderful children and one day we'll add to the family. I so want to give you more sons to carry on your name. Of course, another little girl would be nice, too. All you have to do is get well. Then I will do my part.*

In spite of the shaking and bouncing wagon, the children drifted off to sleep. Ulla put them down on one of the mattresses. Because she didn't know what else she could do, she lay beside Cord so she'd be there if he awakened and needed her.

~ * ~

Cord slept through the day, but Ulla didn't know how. He did grunt every so often when the wagon hit a rut or swayed to the side. When they stopped for the nooning, both Becky and Will were bored and restless. Ivy insisted on taking them to her wagon. She promised to watch them carefully even though she was going to permit Becky to play with Joe.

Saul came to check Cord again and told her he was doing well. He did say she should relax a little and get some rest because Cord's recovery was going to be a slow process and he'd need her even more when he regained consciousness.

She promised she'd try to rest and she was able to do so for a little while. But Cord grew restless and she sat up and checked him.

He opened his eyes and muttered, "I'm sorry, Ulla. I tried my best."

"Cord, you have nothing to be sorry about. You may think Will was hurt, but he wasn't. You save his life by risking your own."

"The limb broke and he began to slip..."

"Shh. Please listen to me, Cord." She had to convince him Will was alive and fine.

He gave her a slight nod and didn't speak.

"Will is fine. You saved his life." She had to make him understand. "He and Becky are with the Nettletons. When we stop for supper, I'll bring them back to our wagon so we can all sleep together."

"Don't lie to me, Ulla. I know what happened."

"I'd never lie to you, Cord. You may think you know what happened when that limb broke, but you don't. You were able to shift to protect Will and in the process you were hurt yourself."

"I hurt, but I should have been the one to die."

"Don't talk like that. The children and I need you and all you have to do is get well for us." She smiled at him. "Now tell me, how do you feel, darling? Do you need medicine for the pain?"

He didn't reply and Ulla knew he'd drifted off to sleep.

The rest of the day's travel was hard on Cord. He continually moaned and groaned, but he never came fully awake. Ulla was glad when they stopped for the night because she knew with the wagon still, he'd be able to rest.

After supper, the children returned to spend the night in the wagon with their mother and father. It comforted Ulla to have them there and she knew it would do Cord good to see Will if and when he awakened again.

It was shortly after the bugle sounded the next morning that Cord opened his eyes for a moment and looked at her. He mumbled a little and she wanted to believe he'd tried to smile at her, but she could have imagined it. She took his hand in hers. She also wanted him to assure her he was going to be all right, though Saul kept telling her he had lots of hope for a recovery. "I'll try to be patient because I know you'll speak to me later, my love. At least I know you are going to wake up."

"Mama," Becky's voice sounded sleepy.

"Yes, sweetheart."

"Is Daddy all right?"

"He just woke up for a minute."

She moved beside he mother. "Can I talk to him?"

"He went back to sleep, but I'm sure he'll be awake soon. You'll be able to talk to him then."

"All right." Becky leaned against her.

"Why don't you lie back down? You need to get as much sleep as you can. I might need your help later and I want you to be rested."

Becky nodded and moved back beside her little brother. Ulla knew it wouldn't take her long to go back to sleep. And it didn't.

There was a light knock on the canvas covering the back of the wagon. Ulla moved to it and pulled it aside. "Good morning, Pete."

"I thought I heard voices in here. Has Cord woken up?"

"He mumbled a few words, but went right back to sleep. I suppose you heard me talking to Becky."

"I see." He nodded at her. "Liam came to get the cow. He said Charlene was going to milk for you and they'd take care of her. Said they'd tie her to his wagon until Cord was better again."

"I hate for her to have to do that."

"Don't worry about it. Ivy and I would've have done it, but they insisted. He also told me Esther is coming to get Becky soon. She says it's a way she can help out since her brother, Eli, has volunteered to drive your wagon."

"I feel…"

"Now, don't start trying to do everything yourself, Ulla. Eli said his folks got along fine without him yesterday and he wanted to drive for you again. You know we all want to help you."

"I know, but I feel I should be doing something."

"Your job is to take care of Cord and nurse him back to health and not to worry about anything else." He held up his hand when she started to speak. "Now, I'm going to hitch up your team and Ivy is preparing breakfast. She said she'd let you know when it was ready."

Ulla didn't have a chance to say anything because Pete gave her a quick smile and hurried away.

~ * ~

They had camped for nooning. Esther had brought Becky to see her mother, but the little girl chose to go back with her friend because Esther had told her they were going to spend some time with Kathleen. Ivy said Will was asleep in the Nettleton wagon. Ulla had not wanted to socialize so she climbed back into her wagon and busied herself mending the clothes Cord had torn on the rocks at the waterfall. She was thinking how much she enjoyed doing this menial task for him when a grunt drew her attention. Laying aside her sewing, she moved closer and leaned over him. "Are you hurting, Cord?"

His eyes opened and he looked at her. Before she could say anything else, he whispered, "I'm so sorry."

"You have nothing to be sorry about. I've already told you, you're a hero in my eyes."

He seemed to ignore her statement. "I honestly tried to save him. I really did. I'm sorry I couldn't."

"You did save Will. He was a little frightened, but otherwise, he's fine."

"Ulla, I know I killed my son."

"Please believe me, Cord. I thought you understood. You didn't hurt Will. I've told you this before, but I'll tell you again. You saved Will's life and put your own in jeopardy. Our son is the same healthy little boy he was before he climbed out on that limb."

"I'm sorry, Ulla. I don't believe you." His eyes began to flutter.

Ulla had to bite her lip to keep from shouting at Cord. Instead, she said in a firm voice, "Don't you dare go back to sleep. I'll be right back."

Cord lifted an eyebrow, but said nothing.

Ulla went to the back of the wagon and waved to Pete who was talking to his wife.

He hurried toward her.

In a matter of minutes, Ivy came running up beside her husband. "Is something wrong, Ulla?"

"No, Ivy. I just want you to bring Will to me. Cord thinks he let the boy die and I need to prove to him that Will is alive and well."

Pete looked surprised. "Cord's awake?"

"He's in and out, but I'm hoping he'll stay awake long enough to see that Will is still with us. I can't convince him otherwise."

"I'll get Will." Ivy hurried to her own wagon.

"Do you want me to get Doc, Ulla? He'd probably like to know that Cord is waking up."

"Yes, but tell him to wait a few minutes to come. I want to talk to Cord alone for a little while."

Pete nodded. "I understand."

In a matter of minutes, Ivy reappeared with a whimpering Will in her arms. "I had to wake him, so he's a little out of sorts."

"He'll be fine." Ulla reached for him. "Come to mama, baby. You can go right back to sleep in a little while."

Will cuddled against her and stopped whimpering as she moved back beside the mattress where Cord lay. She was disappointed to see his eyes closed. "Cord," she said gently to make sure he was asleep again.

He was.

"Oh Will, we're going to have to wait until your daddy wakes up again." She held the little boy close and rocked him. He soon fell back to sleep and she lay him on the other mattress, then picked up her sewing. She decided she would keep Will with her until she could prove to Cord his son hadn't been harmed. Then she'd send someone for Becky. She wanted her whole family together.

Thirteen

They had camped for the night when Cord opened his eyes. For a few minutes he couldn't understand why every part of his body hurt. Then he remembered the waterfall. It was as if he could feel his son's trusting little arms around his neck and hear him say, "Hey, Daddy." He didn't remember if he said anything back to the little boy because he was concentrating on getting the child safely to the river bank and into Ulla's waiting arms.

But he had failed. Failed miserably.

He felt the baby slipping from his arms then everything went black. Now here he lay with probably more than one broken bone in his body and if they hadn't fished his body out of the water, his precious son was somewhere on those jagged rocks at the bottom of the falls.

Why couldn't he exchange places with Will? Why couldn't he have been the one to hit those rocks at the bottom of the falls instead of his son? Why was the one who didn't deserve to live still alive when the precious child had died?

In spite of all he could do, a tear rolled down Cord's face. "Oh, God if I could do it over, I'd do it so differently. I'd be like Ulla. I'd love little Will and let him know it's because he's a wonderful little boy no matter whose seed brought him into being."

His hand moved and he was startled to feel someone beside him. He frowned. It couldn't be Ulla. There was no way she would want to be this near him. She had to hate him for letting Will die.

She jerked up and he thought she was trying to get away from him.

"Oh, Cord. You're awake." Lighting the lantern, she set it beside the mattress and leaned over him. Her face was close to his. "How are you feeling?"

He didn't answer her question, but said, "I'm so sorry, Ulla. Please believe me. I tried to save him.

"Listen to me, Cord. I know you think Will fell, but he didn't. You managed to shelter him and he's fine. You were the only one hurt."

"Don't lie to me, Ulla."

"Now listen to me. I've told you before…I have never lied to you and I never will." She turned her back and leaned in the other direction. When she turned back to him, she had Will in her arms. "See. Here is Will. He's perfectly fine."

Cord looked confused. "How?"

"You managed to hold him away from harm and when they pulled you to the shore, they had to pry him out of your protective arms. You weren't about to let him go."

Will stirred and opened his eyes.

"Will…" Cord could barely say the name without choking up.

Will looked around and saw his father. He grinned and reached out to him. Ulla leaned him down and Will patted Cord's face. "Daddy fall."

Cord stared at the little boy. "Am I dreaming?"

"No, Cord. You're not dreaming. Will is safe and he doesn't have a scratch on him. It's all thanks to your quick actions."

"What happened?"

Will's head fell forward against Ulla's chest and he looked as if he couldn't keep his eyes open.

"Let me put him back on the mattress so he can go back to sleep and I'll tell you."

"If you don't mind, put him down here beside me so I can look at him."

Ulla smiled and lay Will close to his daddy. Cord smiled back at her then at the little boy as if he still couldn't believe the child was alive. "I'm ready now to hear what happened after I was fell."

~*~

Ulla and the children walked up to the campfire at the nooning. "I feel bad about not helping you do the cooking, Ivy. Especially in..."

Ivy interrupted her. "Don't be silly. You have your hands full looking after Cord and the children. When he is well, I'm sure you'll be making those biscuits for all of us."

"I sure will."

"Has Cord awakened again?"

"He was for a little bit while we were moving, but I think the jarring of the wagon kept him in pain. I gave him a dose of laudanum and he went back to sleep. He woke up when we stopped, but he was drowsy so I decided to get the children out of the wagon so he could rest while we were here."

"At least he's awake and talking, isn't he?"

"He is, but I'm still concerned about him, Ivy."

"But you said..."

"I know. I told you I finally convinced him Will was alive, but he fell back to sleep before I could tell him everything that happened after his fall."

"I'm sure that's a good sign. He'll probably stay awake longer next time." She poured milk for the children. Becky took hers and the plate Ivy handed her and joined Joe on the ground near the wagon.

Ulla looked back into the wagon and smiled. "He has drifted off."

Ivy nodded. "I bet you're ready for coffee?"

Will patted his mother's face. "Coffee."

The women laughed.

Ulla hugged him to her. "No, baby. You're too young for coffee. You're drinking milk."

"Milk."

"That's right, little man. Milk." Ivy smiled at him and handed his mother a plate filled with a vegetable stew.

Ulla took a seat in one of the chairs and began feeding Will. "I thought Cord would stay awake for longer periods now that he seems to have come to himself. That's why I can't help being concerned."

Before Ivy could answer, Pete walked up and his wife turned to fix a plate for him. "Well, ladies, we may be camping here longer than we thought."

"What's going on, honey?"

"Some men rode up looking for a doctor. Seems there was a tornado that almost destroyed the nearby town a few days ago. Several people were killed, including their doctor. A lot more people were hurt, some critically. They've been waiting for a wagon train that might have a doctor or somebody with medical knowledge who would come to help them out."

"And of course, Saul being the wonderful man he is, he went to help," Ulla added.

"He did. Mr. Pruitt also went with him to assess the situation." He sipped the coffee Ivy handed him. "How's Cord? Has he woke up again?"

"He did, but he's asleep again. I just told Ivy how he's been moaning and groaning while we were moving. I was hoping Saul would check him while we were camped."

"Maybe Naomi would come check him. She's a good nurse," Pete suggested.

Ulla nodded. "That's a good idea."

He sat his plate down. "I'll go get her."

Ivy put her hand on his arm. "I'll go as soon as I pack up, dear. I'll take Becky and Joe with me. They might like to play with their friends."

"Thank you, Ivy." Ulla ate a few bites and set her plate down. "I'll go check on Cord. I don't want him waking up and not finding me there."

"I'll help you into the wagon, Ulla."

"Thank you, Pete."

"Ulla, let me make Cord a plate. If he awakes, he should try to eat something and I think the broth of this stew would be good for him."

"That's a good idea. Thank you." Ulla smiled at her. "It seems all I do is thank you, my friends."

"You know you don't have to thank us, Ulla. By bringing us on this journey, you've more than earned anything we could ever do to repay you." He held Will as she climbed into the wagon, then handed him to her. "You take care of your husband and baby and I think I'll go walk Ivy to the Guggenheim wagon."

~ * ~

Ivy finished putting away the noon supplies and called the children to come. They responded immediately. "I'll be back in a bit, Pete," she said to her husband.

"I think I'll walk with you." He winked at her. "Sometimes I just want to have an excuse to hold my wife's hand."

She blushed. "Pete, sometimes you say the sweetest things."

Joe and Becky were walking a few steps in front of them, but they heard Joe say, "Sometimes Mama and Daddy say silly things like that, Becky."

"My mama and daddy do it, too. Mama keeps telling Daddy how much she wants him to get well so they can have more babies." She shook her head. "I don't think they need anybody 'cept Will and me, but I guess they think they do."

"Sometimes I wish my mama would have another baby."

Becky looked up at him as if she couldn't believe he said such a thing. "Why?"

"Cause she's always hugging and kissing on me and if there was a baby maybe she wouldn't do it so much."

"Don't you like her hugging and kissing on you?"

"Sometimes, but it's embarrassing in front of other people."

"I like for Mama and Daddy to hug and kiss me."

"You're a girl."

"So what's the matter with that?"

They moved further ahead and Ivy looked up at Pete, shaking her head.

He laughed and squeezed her hand. "I think Joe might have a good idea. I wouldn't mind having another little Nettleton in the family."

Ivy bit her lip. "Are you serious?"

"Of course I am. When we get settled, I don't see any reason why we shouldn't add to our family. We're still young enough and Joe shouldn't grow up alone. Besides, I've seen you with Will. You're a wonderful mother."

Ivy didn't answer.

Pete frowned. "Did I say something wrong?"

"Oh, no, darling."

"Then what is it? I can tell something isn't right.

She shook her head. "No, Pete. There's nothing wrong. That is, with the exception that I have something I need to tell you."

He stopped and looked down at her. His face was full of concern. "What is it?"

She turned toward him and smiled. "It's time I let you know our second child should arrive in about six and a half months."

A myriad of emotions crossed his face as he stared at her. Finally he whispered, "Are you sure?"

"Yes, darling. I'm positive."

Pete dropped her hand and swept her into his arms. He kissed her passionately. "Oh, Ivy. That's wonderful news. I love you so."

"I love you, too, my husband. I have always loved you."

As if he suddenly thought of something, a frown crossed Pete's face and he held her from him. "Wait just a minute. Did you say six and a half months?"

She nodded.

He took on a worried look. "Then that means you were with child before we left Independence, doesn't it?"

She nodded again.

"Did you know?"

She sighed. "Yes, Pete. I knew."

"Why didn't you tell me?"

"Would you have come on this trip if I'd told you?"

"Of course not."

"That's what I thought and I wanted us to come, Pete. Our family needed a new start and you must admit we've all been happy since leaving."

"Yes, but...."

"No, Pete. I know in my heart that it was the right thing to do. Look how Joe has come out and is making friends. In Independence he stayed to himself all the time and only played with Springer. Now he is coming into his own."

"But..."

"There you go again with that word 'but.' Now stop it and think. Look how many friends we've made on this wagon train. Of those who know you've been in prison, none of them hold your past against you."

"I know all that, Ivy. I just want you to be safe and it's my duty to protect you."

She laughed. "Honey, women have had babies for thousands of years. Everything will be fine. Just you wait and see."

"I'll try to believe that, but I can't help worrying." He kissed her again.

Joe and Becky came back to where they were standing. "Please, Dad. Stop kissing Mama and let's go. I want to see if Carney can play with us."

Pete chuckled. "We're coming, son."

Joe turned back to Becky. "I ain't never going to get married if you have to kiss on an old girl like he does Mama."

"I ain't going to let no ole boy ever kiss on me like that," Becky replied.

"Then maybe you and me will get married when we're old like them."

"I don't know if I want to marry you or not."

They drifted away and Ivy giggled. As she locked her arm in Pete's, she said. "I hope Joe's idea of marriage will eventually change."

"Don't worry, sweetheart. It'll change. Just give him a few years and we'll have to tie him down to keep him away from the girls. After all, he takes after his old man."

Ivy gave him a playful punch on the arm and they walked forward.

~ * ~

Naomi did come to check Cord and help Ulla change the bandage on his hip. "Boy, he's got one whopper of a birth mark on that hip, doesn't he?" Naomi observed.

Ulla didn't want to say it was the first time she'd seen it. Instead she said, "Will has one, too."

"Then it must run in the family."

"Maybe it does." Ulla still looked concerned. "I hope Cord's going to be all right."

"Now stop worrying so much. He's doing as well as could be expected with the injuries he has," Naomi said. "Since we've changed the bandage, you probably won't have to do it again until tomorrow."

"Thank you, Naomi."

"I see you have that food there, so do your best to get it in him. He needs to build up his strength."

"I'll do it."

"Now you get some rest yourself, my friend. You look as if you can use it."

"I'll try."

"Good."

"As for the food, Cord did take a bite or two before he went to sleep again. I'll see that he eats when he wakes up again."

"You do that, and don't hesitate to send for me if you need me. Saul is still in that little town, but he should be back soon."

"Thank you, Naomi."

~ * ~

It was supper when Cord awakened again.

Will sat on the mattress beside him watching Ulla spoon the stew broth into Cord's mouth.

"Daddy eat."

"Yes, baby. Daddy eat."

Cord swallowed. "You want to eat with Daddy, Will?"

"I eat."

"We'll eat in a minute, sweetheart. This is for your daddy."

"My son looks hungry. Let him have a bite, Ulla."

She smiled at Cord and held a spoonful of soup out to the little boy. "Here you go, honey."

He ate it and laughed.

She turned to Cord. "Now that you've discovered what a wonderful son you have, don't you start spoiling him."

"I won't..." he took another bite, "...not much anyway."

Ulla chuckled. "I was afraid of that."

"Excuse me, Ulla." Pete's voice came through the back of the wagon. "Ivy wanted to know if you needed any more stew for Cord."

She looked at Cord. "Could you eat some more?"

He shook his head. "Not right now. I'm full."

"No, thanks, Pete. Maybe I can get him to eat more later."

"If he feels like company, I'd like to come in and talk for a bit."

Before Ulla could answer, Cord said, "Come on in, Pete. Since Becky has left to eat, Ulla needs to get out of here to feed Will and eat supper herself."

"I could wait, but I think this little fellow is hungry." She patted Cord's shoulder. "Don't you overdo now. If you get tired and need him to go, Pete will understand."

"I sure will, Ulla." He reached to help her out of the wagon, picked up Will and handed him to his mother.

As soon as Ulla had moved away from the wagon, Pete climbed in and took a seat beside Cord. "How are you really feeling?"

Cord shook his head. "Like hell, man. Every part of my body aches."

"It's no wonder. You may not know it, but you were almost killed."

"Naomi said I was in pretty bad shape, but told me Saul says he thinks I'll make it."

"Did she tell you Saul said traveling in the wagon was going to make your progress slower?"

"She mentioned that I should get as comfortable as I could." Cord gave Pete a hard look. "I have a feeling you've got something besides my comfort on your mind. What is it, Pete?"

"Did Ulla tell you the reason we stayed camped here after the nooning break was because of a town that's been almost destroyed and needed a doctor for their wounded?"

"She mentioned it."

"I was with the livestock when Pruitt came back. He said it was worse than he imagined. Not only are there destroyed buildings, but some families have had their lives torn apart. It's going to take a lot of work and an influx of new families to build Winton Crossing back to what it used to be."

"I'm sorry for those people. I know what it's like to lose everything you own and have to start over."

"I guess that in a way I do, too. But I never lost the most important things to me."

"Oh?"

"I never lost Ivy or Joe. They're more precious than any amount of material things."

Cord nodded. "Of course, you're right. I still have my children and I have Ulla. With them, I suppose I could start over again many times."

"I feel the same way."

"I know you do, Pete, but what has that got to do with what you wanted to talk to me about?"

"Nothing, I guess. What I really wanted to tell you is that I'm going to be a father again."

Cord smiled. "Congratulations. You happy about it?"

"Very. I'm just concerned about Ivy."

"She's all right, isn't she?"

"As far as I know, but she's working awfully hard and, well, you never know, but anything could happen."

"I'm sorry, Pete. That's my fault." Cord tried to sit up. "I'll get out of this bed ..."

"No, Cord. I didn't mean that. I mean this whole trip has been hard for her. She won't admit it, but I'm afraid it'll be too much if we try to make it all the way to Oregon."

"Well, Pete, if you feel you need to pull out..."

"No, Cord. Ivy would never stand for that and to be honest, neither would I. Remember the fight we had about it earlier? Of course, Ivy was right. Ulla has been awfully good to us and there's no way we would let her down if she really wants to go to Oregon."

"It wasn't Ulla's idea to go to Oregon. It was mine."

Pete nodded. "I thought so. That's why I wanted to run my idea by you."

Cord lifted an eyebrow. "What's your idea?"

"Well, Ulla told us how hard the wagon ride has been on you today and since Ivy is with child, what would you think of our two families settling in Winton Crossing?"

Cord frowned. "Is that the same town Pruitt was talking about a while back?"

"I think it could have been. Did you happen to mention it to Ulla?"

"I don't think so, Pete. Why do you ask?"

"If the wives agree, I feel it might be a good solution for our families."

"It sure would be an answer for both of us. You wouldn't worry so much about Ivy and I sure wouldn't mind giving up riding in this wagon until I can at least walk again."

"That's what I thought."

"Tell you what, Pete. Why don't you take a ride to the town and see if you think it's a good place to settle? Meantime, I'll discuss it with Ulla and see if she would be willing to give up going to Oregon."

"Sounds good. It's still a while before the sun sets, so I'll head out there now if you don't mind me using your horse."

"Of course, I don't mind."

"Thanks." Pete stood. "By the way, it's good to see you doing so well. Had my doubts about your recovery for a while there."

"Thanks, Pete. I guess you weren't the only one who thought that. I just hope it won't be too long before I can get out of this bed and pull my weight again."

"With the care your wife is giving you, I'm sure it'll be sooner than you think."

Cord watched him climb out of the wagon and let his words sink into his mind. He was right. Ulla had been wonderful to look after him as she had. He wondered if she did it because she cared enough to do so or if it was because she needed him.

Talking with Pete had tired him more than he thought it would and he began to feel drowsy. His mind began to drift. *Though I hope she's nursing me because she cares, I'm pretty sure it's because she needs me for this trip.* As he drifted off to sleep, he muttered, "Maybe it's a little of both and that gives me hope for our future together."

Fourteen

The children had fallen asleep and Ulla was sure Cord was close to it. She wasn't so sure about herself. Now that they'd made the decision to pull out of the wagon train and settle in Winton Crossing, she should feel more relief, but for some reason she didn't. What if Cord decided it wasn't what he really wanted? What if he blamed her for encouraging him to abandon the idea of going to Oregon when he realized he didn't like this small Wyoming town? Of course she knew it was the right thing for him now. Traveling farther could cause permanent damage to his already bruised and battered body, but would he remember that when he was well and able to do the things he wanted or needed to do again?

Yes, Mr. Pruitt said if they changed their minds and wanted to go on further west, they could join the next wagon train that came by. And according to him, there would be several in the next month or so. Then more would come through the following year. Surely they would know if they were satisfied to live in Winton Crossing by then.

Glancing toward him in the dark, she wanted to reach out and touch him, but stopped herself. She was next to his uninjured side, but she was afraid he'd wake up and wonder why she was so close. She risked moving a little closer to him and was surprised when he whispered, "Can't you sleep, Ulla?"

"I'll eventually go to sleep."

"Are you upset because I agreed with Pete that we should leave the wagon train?"

"Not at all. I just know when I first met you, you said you intended to go to Oregon and now we're going to live in Wyoming. I want to be sure it's what you really want to do."

"What I wanted all along is to get away from Atlanta and start a new life with my children. I chose Oregon because that is where the wagon trains seemed to be headed. Wyoming Territory seems to be a good place, too. According to Pete, it can be a nice little town with some work. It will be as easy to start over here as it will be in Oregon."

"Then, if you're happy about the change, so am I."

She felt his hand touch her shoulder. "If you're always going to be this agreeable with my decisions, then we're going to have a long happy marriage."

She laughed. "Oh, Cord. You can't always count on my agreeing with you about everything. I can get pretty opinionated at times."

He let go of her hand and the next thing she knew he'd slipped his arm around her shoulder and pulled her closer to him. "I wouldn't want you any other way, Ulla."

"I'm glad, because I probably won't be changing a lot."

He chuckled and squeezed her a little tighter. "If I wasn't in such bad shape, I'd … well, never mind. We'll discuss it later."

Ulla bit her lip. Was he inferring what she thought he was? Dare she say something to let him know she understood? Why not? "Maybe you won't be in bad shape much longer."

"It sounds like you might be ready to be married to me in more ways than just in name." When she didn't say anything, he asked, "How about it? Will you be my wife in all ways, Ulla?"

She took a deep breath. "Yes, Cord. I'm ready to be your wife."

"That gives me more incentive than Saul's pills. I'm going to start getting well in a hurry."

"I'm glad I inspire you."

He pulled her closer and she cuddled against him. She was getting sleepy, but a thought crossed her mind. "May I ask you something, Cord?"

"You can ask me anything."

"Tell me about that birthmark on your hip."

"How did you know about that?"

"I helped Naomi change a bandage on it earlier today."

"Something about that doesn't seem fair."

She frowned. "What do you mean?"

"You've seen my hip and I've never seen yours."

She blushed, but knew he couldn't see her. "Seems fair to me. Now tell me about the birthmark."

"Not much to tell. My dad had one and so did my brother. Dad told us it was the mark of the Dermott men. Why did you want to know about it, anyway?"

"Have you ever looked at Will's hip?"

"No. Why should I?"

She chuckled. "You'd have saved yourself some agony and questions about your son if you had."

"Why...wait a minute. Are you saying Will has a birthmark on his hip?"

"Yes, Cord, I am. I guess that means he has the mark of the Dermott men, too."

"Then that proves...."

"Yes, Cord. It proves beyond doubt that you're Will's birth father."

He was silent for a moment, then said, "I'm pleased to know he is my natural son because that means there's no doubt who fathered him. You may not believe this, Ulla, but it doesn't make me love him any more than I already do. When I saw him on that limb about to plunge to his death, I knew I loved him as much as any father ever could love their child."

"I'm glad you feel that way because he sure loves you."

Cord tilted her head toward his and kissed her. "I swore I'd never love another beautiful woman as long as I lived, but I was so wrong. I love you, Ulla. I think I fell in love with you the moment you popped up from behind that counter in Wingate's Store and looked at me with those beautiful green eyes."

"Oh, Cord. I had feelings for you the instant I looked into your chest and let my eyes drift to your handsome face. I just wouldn't admit it because I thought you were a married man."

"Oh, Ulla. I can't wait until I can make love to my wife." He kissed her again. This time with more passion. He then let out a groan.

"Slow down, my husband. You know you have to heal before things can go any further between us."

"I know, but maybe Saul has some kind of magic pill that will make me heal faster."

Ulla giggled, kissed his cheek, then snuggled down with her head on his right shoulder. "I'll ask the doctor tomorrow, my love. Now relax and let's go to sleep."

"Relax, she says, when all I want to do is ..."

"I know what you want to do, but it's impossible at this moment. Now let's try to get some rest. We'll be moving to our new home tomorrow."

"If you insist." He pulled her tighter.

Ulla smiled into the dark, glad she didn't say what she was thinking because she couldn't wait until his injuries healed, either.

Epilogue

Stuart Roberson walked into the bank with a stack of letters in his hand. "Wilbur, let Henry take care of the customers and come into my office for a minute, please."

Wilbur looked surprised and a little confused, but only nodded and followed his boss.

In the office, Stuart said, "Sit down. This won't take long."

"Have I done something wrong, Mr. Roberson?"

"Of course not, Wilbur, and I thought we agreed that you'd call me Stuart."

Wilbur visually relaxed. "Yes, we did. I'm sorry."

"No need to be sorry." He waved a letter in the air. "I heard from Ulla and I was sure you'd want to hear what she had to say."

"I absolutely would. How is she?"

"I haven't read the letter yet, so we'll find out together." He ripped open the letter and began to read aloud:

Dear Papa Stuart,
I hope this letter finds you well and still prospering in your bank.
I promised to let you know how things are going with me when

we were settled for good. My family and I decided to build our home in Wyoming instead of Oregon. Pete Nettleton had heard about a good little town in the territory and he was right. Cord had been injured and traveling became hard for him so we branched off the wagon train and settled in the nice little town of Winton Crossing. Though it had been through a devastating storm, the people there had strong beliefs that it would build back up and become a prosperous place again. They were right. Moving here was a good decision for us. We took the wheels off our wagon and planned to live in it until we could build a house. Then, as if it was destined, the couple who ran the small store in town decided they were getting too old to rebuild and run the business any longer. I was thrilled when they decided to sell because you know how much I enjoyed running the store in Independence.

When I decided to buy the place, I told Cord about my money. As I expected, he refused to see it as ours. He said he wanted to provide for his wife and children and had enough for us to live on. It took a lot to convince him to use any of my money, but after I assured him I'd let him pay me back, he relented and we bought the store. After acquiring the store, we didn't have to build a house right away. There were three rooms upstairs that worked perfectly for us for a while, though Cord is building a home for us on the street behind the store as I write this letter. He says he doesn't want to raise our children without a yard to play in. Though I loved living in our little apartment with him and the children, I admit I'm looking forward to our house.

I know you had no way of knowing, but Cord worked for a newspaper in Atlanta. He has bought the building next door to the store and is working on opening a newspaper office for our town. Everyone here is excited about it. I was pleased that he insisted on putting a door in his building connecting it to the store, in case I need him.

Two other families and the Nettletons have settled here, too and we're very pleased by that. Ivy has opened a sweet shop down the street and as I'm sure you can guess, she has a booming business.

They didn't want to accept a loan from me to do it, but I insisted and they've had no trouble paying me back. Cord says the best part of the deal is that Ivy insists that she give us a cake or pie each week as interest on the money. And would you believe, Pete has been elected sheriff? Though most people know about his past, it didn't seem to matter after he caught an outlaw trying to steal from some of the people whose houses were partially torn up. The townspeople love him and of course their son, Joe, is as proud as he can be of his father. I'm sure their four-month-old daughter will be just as proud when she grows up.

Ivy didn't tell any of us that she was with child when we left Independence. Her baby was the first child born in town after the terrible storm and of course, she became the darling of Winton Crossing. Pete was beside himself and was so overprotective that Ivy had a hard time telling him she could still do the cooking and other duties we women have to do.

The other couples who decided to settle here with us were Saul Guggenheim and his family, and Liam Mahoney and his.

Saul is a doctor and because there were so many people hurt in the storm, he felt he was needed here more than he was in Oregon.

Liam Mahoney is Winton Crossing's first lawyer and has recently been elected mayor. Needless to say, he and his family are well respected, too.

Our children are growing and thriving. Becky is doing great in her school work. She's such a smart little girl. Everyone is amazed that she's already reading and can do simple arithmetic. Will has grown into an even more precious little boy. He thinks he can read, too, though he often holds his book upside down.

There will be another little Dermott in the summer. Cord is acting the same way Pete did. He thinks I'm going to hurt myself if I pick up a can of beans. I send him to his newspaper office when he hovers too much, but of course I love the attention from the man I married. I was so lucky to meet him at just the right time in my life. We have fallen deeply in love and I know we have a wonderful life ahead of us.

Please tell Wilbur that I think of you two often. You were my best friends and I miss you terribly, but marrying Cord and leaving Independence was the best thing I've ever done. I never dreamed a woman could be as happy as I am. I wouldn't change my life with my husband and children for anything. I'm sure that my parents would be happy at the way things have turned out for me, too.

I've heard rumors that there will be a railroad coming to our town in the near future. If so, I hope both of you will consider coming for a visit. I would enjoy seeing you and I want you to know that you're welcome to visit anytime you can.

Your adopted daughter,
Ulla.

Stuart folded the letter and took a deep breath. "I'm so glad she's happy."

"So am I." Wilbur discreetly rubbed his watery eyes.

"I'm going to write her back and tell her that I may take her up on her invitation to visit. I don't know if I can wait for the railroad to be finished. I might be too old when it's done. But there are other ways to travel."

Wilbur stood. "Thank you for sharing her letter with me, Stuart. When you write back, please tell her I said I miss her, and my family and I are still thankful for telling me about this job. I'll also have my wife write to her from us."

"I'm sure Ulla will like that, Wilbur." He watched Wilbur leave the office. *Wilbur may think he's the lucky one, but I think it's the other way round. I've never had an employee as devoted and hard working as he is. I'm telling him at the last of the week about the raise and the promotion I've decided to give him. And as soon as he learns his new duties, I'm heading to Winton Crossing, Wyoming.*

~ * ~

Ulla turned from dusting the canned food on the shelf as the bell over the door jangled and the stage driver and two passengers stepped inside.

"Got some mail for you, Miz Dermott."

"Thank you, Silas." She put her feather duster down and turned.

Silas handed her a stack of mail and turned to leave to rest and water the horses pulling the stage.

She smiled at the man and woman who came in. "I hope you folks are having a good trip."

"It's a little tiring," the woman said.

"Did I see the sign of a sweet shop down the street?" the man asked.

"Yes, and their pastries are wonderful."

"I thought so. The other man on the stage said that was where he was headed first. Let's go down there, Mable. I want something sweet."

"We'll be back." They left the store and headed toward Ivy's Sweet Shop.

Cord came in from the back. "I heard the stage come in and thought I'd check on you. How are you, sweetheart?"

"I'm fine. How about you?"

He laughed. "Well, if you must know, I mashed my finger with the hammer while I was nailing that shelf up you wanted in your new kitchen."

"Oh, I'm so sorry. Come here and I'll kiss it like I do Will when he hurts himself."

"I think my finger will survive, but I'll let you give me the kiss on my lips if I can figure out how to hurt them."

"Cord, you're awful."

"Nope. I'm just a man who loves his wife."

She shook her head and picked up the mail to sort for the townspeople who would be coming by to see if they got anything. "The stage will be pulling away soon...see if you can control yourself until then."

He winked at her. "I'll try."

Instead of continuing the banter with him, she let out a little cry. "Oh, Cord. I have a letter from Mr. Roberson." She ripped it open and began to read:

Dear Ulla,

You'll never know how much your letter meant to Wilbur and me. I'm sorry it took me so long to write back, but I did want to let you know what all is going on in Independence. Wilbur said he and his wife will write you, too. They may have already.

First, let me say I'm so glad you have found a happy life with a good man and the children. I know you're excited to be adding to your family. I'm anxious to find out if I'm going to have a 'grandson' or a 'granddaughter.' Whatever it is, I'm sure it'll not lack for love.

Things are going well at the bank. I'm pleased with the way Wilbur has worked out. He's done such a good job that I've promoted him from teller to my assistant. I'm grooming him so he can take over and run things whenever I find I can take a trip west to visit my 'substitute daughter' and her family.

I thought you might be interested to know there is no longer a Wingate's General Store in operation here in town, but there is a nice place called Booker's Store. When Alton Wingate and his wife let the store fail, they finally gave up and sold it. They also sold your old house to the Bookers. It would please you to see that Milton and Lavern Booker have restored the house to its former beauty. Just the way it was when your mother and father were alive.

As for your Uncle Alton and Aunt Vida, they packed up and moved away. I'm not sure where, and Claudine said she didn't know because they hadn't written her. I know it will surprise you to learn that after her parents left, Claudine and her husband have settled on a little farm outside of town. This may be hard for you to believe, but they've turned into a settled hard working couple. Colton took right to farming and the baby, a boy, has a good home. I told her about your letter and she asked me if it would be all right to write to you. She said she wanted to apologize for the way she and her folks treated you. I told her I thought you'd be pleased to hear from her. If you're not, just burn her letter.

I will close for now, but don't be surprised if I show up in that store of yours looking for the home of Mr. and Mrs. Cord Dermott sometime in the near future. Hug the children and...

My best to you,
Papa Stuart

"Oh, Cord." She turned to him with tears in her eyes."

He rushed to his wife and folded his arms around her. "What's wrong, darling?"

"I'm so happy."

He took a breath. "Happy? I thought something terrible had happened."

She shook her head. "Don't you know a woman sometimes cries when she's happy?"

"If you say so."

She crammed the letter in his hand. "Read this and you'll understand."

After reading the letter, he again took her in his arms. "I love you, Ulla and I hope Mr. Roberson decides to visit us soon."

"Oh, I do, too. He'd be the perfect ..."

The bell over the door jangled and Becky came in. She held her brother's hand with her left and a businessman's hand in her right. "Oh my, they're kissing again," she said. "They do that all the time."

Pulling apart they both looked at her when she added, "I found this man outside. He says he's our grandpa. Is he, Mama?"

For a moment, Ulla was stunned. Then she let out a little cry and ran to the man. Throwing her arms around his neck, she cried, "Oh, Papa Stuart, I just read your letter."

"Almost beat it here, didn't I?"

"Oh, it's so good to see you."

Cord walked up and held out his hand. "Mr. Roberson, let me add my welcome to my wife's greeting."

He shook Cord's hand. "Good to see you again, Cord, and please drop the Mr. Roberson. According to Becky, I'm the only grandpa the children have and I think we should be on a first name basis."

"I agree, Stuart."

"I see you have done right by little Ulla. She looks awfully happy."

"I'm not so little now, but oh how happy I am." She gasped.

"Why are your frowning, Mama?"

"No reason, Becky. I think...." she gasped again and grabbed her stomach. "Honey, go get Doctor Guggenheim and take Will to Miss Ivy. I think we're going to need their help today."

"Okay, Mama." She took her brother's hand and looked up at her father and in a very grown-up voice, said, "You take care of Mama until I get back with the doctor."

Cord looked puzzled, but muttered, "Of course I will, Becky."

"I'm sorry," Ulla said. "I think I ... oh..." She grabbed her stomach again.

"What the hell is going on?" Cord asked.

"I think you're about to become a father again, Cord," Stuart said.

"I know that. The baby is due in June."

Ulla reached for his hand. "Honey, it's June the fourth. Now, help me upstairs. I think I should go to bed."

"Why?"

Stuart took over. "For heaven's sake, Cord. Your wife is about to give birth. Now get a grip on yourself and help Ulla to bed. I'll take care of the store and wait for my newest grandchild to be born." He began to hum. "Couldn't have come to town at a better time, could I?"

~ * ~

Six hours later the cry of a child sounded and Cord jumped up from the chair at the small table where he was having coffee with Stuart.

Saul Guggenheim came into the room. "Cord, I'm sorry to disappoint Becky, but you have a healthy baby boy and Ulla is doing fine. You can see them both as soon as my wife gets them cleaned up."

In a matter of minutes, Cord joined his wife. He hurried to the bed, leaned down and kissed her on the forehead. "How are you feeling, darling?"

"I'm tired, but I'm happy. Now what do you think of your new son?"

He grinned at the squirming wrinkled baby lying at her side. "He's great, Ulla. You did a wonderful job getting him here."

"I'm glad you like him because I think he's kind of special, too." She gave him a tired, but happy smile. "Would you object if we named him Grady after my father?"

"I think Grady is a wonderful name and a good way to honor your father."

"Thank you, my love." She glanced at her son. "I hope Becky isn't too disappointed because she kept saying she wanted a little sister."

"Once she sees her new brother, she'll be proud to have him."

"Maybe I can have a girl for her next time."

"So you plan to have another one?"

"Of course. You will cooperate, won't you?"

He grinned at her. "I can't wait to cooperate." He dropped to the side of the bed and kissed her again. "There's someone else who'll be here to help us raise them, too."

Ulla frowned. "Who?"

"Their grandpa."

"What are you talking about?"

"While we were waiting for our little boy, Stuart told me he'd made plans to move his banking business here and set up a bank because Winton Crossing is now big enough to support one. He plans to hire Wilber to run the bank in Independence for him."

"Why in the world would he do that?"

"Well, the way he explained it to me, he says he wants to be near his family. And to him, you, and now the children and me are his family."

Ulla grinned. "It'll be nice to have him here."

"He plans to help me finish the house, then he wants to move into this apartment. He says that way he'll always be near if we need him."

"Oh, Cord, that's good news." She began to nod.

Cord eased his arm around her shoulders. "You're getting sleepy, my love. I'm going to get the children so they can meet their new brother, then you can sleep."

"Don't leave me. Let Papa Stuart bring the children."

"I'll do that."

Cord slipped her head to the pillow and stood. Walking to the other side of the bed, he picked up his son. Staring at the little boy he whispered, "I'm glad your mama named you Grady, son. It's a fine name and you'll wear it proudly."

He walked to the door and opened it. Naomi sat in a chair near the bedroom door. "Send Stuart to get the children, Naomi. Ulla asked me to stay in the bedroom with her and I'm going to do it. There's nothing I'd not do for my wife as long as it's in my power to do it."

"You're a thoughtful husband. Just to let you know, the children are already here."

"Then send them in so they can see their brother. Also ask Stuart to come with them."

Naomi frowned. "Who is that man, Cord?"

"He's Ulla's substitute father so that makes him family."

"Good to know, especially since Becky is calling him Grandpa."

Cord grinned. Maybe his children hadn't had much love from the grandparents in Atlanta, but he was sure they'd have it now.

He looked back at his wife, heard Stuart and the children coming and whispered, "Thank you, God. I feel like I'm the luckiest man in the world because Ulla Wingate had the courage to marry a mixed-up bitter stranger and with Your help turn him into a happy, happy man."

Meet Agnes Alexander

Agnes Alexander is a multi-published author with over 40 books in print. She writes in different genres, but says her favorite to write is the Western Historical Romance. Her first WHR was published in 2012. Since then she has had 13 in print. With the publication of *Ulla's Courage*, she'll have 14. She's now busy working on number 15.

As well as writing, Agnes enjoys working with serious new writers and has helped four unpublished writers see their books in print. But if you ask her what she enjoys best, she will tell you her most favorite thing to do is spend time with her two grandchildren.

Other Works From The Pen Of

Agnes Alexander

Valissa's Home – Penniless, after her brother gambles away everything they own, Valissa has to cope with the big cowboy who now owns her home.

Opal's Faith – In the West, Opal's family not only has to adjust to the strangeness of the land, but cope with a neighbor who is making slaves of young boys.

Letter to Our Readers

Enjoy this book?

You can make a difference

As an independent publisher, Wings ePress, Inc. does not have the financial clout of the large New York Publishers. We can't afford large magazine spreads or subway posters to tell people about our quality books.

But, we do have something much more effective and powerful than ads. We have a large base of loyal readers.

Honest Reviews help bring the attention of new readers to our books.

If you enjoyed this book, we would appreciate it if you would spend a few minutes posting a review on the site where you purchased this book or on the Wings ePress, Inc. webpages at: https://wingsepress.com/

Visit Our Website

For The Full Inventory
Of Quality Books:

Wings ePress.Inc
https://wingsepress.com/

Quality trade paperbacks and downloads
in multiple formats,
in genres ranging from light romantic comedy
to general fiction and horror.
Wings has something for every reader's taste.
Visit the website, then bookmark it.
We add new titles each month!

Wings ePress Inc.
3000 N. Rock Road
Newton, KS 67114